THIRST TRAP

CHELLE SLOAN

D1707573

CWR PUBLISHING, LLC

Cover Design: Kari March Designs

Line editing: Marla Selkow Esposito, Proofing with Style

Proofreading: Michele Ficht

DEDICATION

To the #ThirstTrap Squad and my 400K plus friends on
TikTok…

This is for you. Stay hydrated. And thank you for making this
past year unforgettable.

1

WHITLEY

"WOOO!"

I lift my glass as my legs continue to pedal as we take yet another shot in honor of Ella Mae, the bride-to-be and my former sorority sister at Alabama.

"I'm getting married!" she yells, nearly falling off her seat. Somehow, despite the fact that I'm just as drunk as she is, I reach out an arm to make sure she doesn't fall off the pedal tavern.

Pretty good for a former beauty queen from Birmingham. Whoever thought it was a good idea to let a group of drunk bachelorettes ride around on a bar on wheels needs their head examined.

"Thanks, Whitley," Ella Mae says, putting her head on my shoulder. Somehow her feet are still on the pedals, which is actually pretty impressive.

"Anytime," I say, trying to help her sit up. "You better drink some water, we have a long night still to go."

"That's right we do!" Betsy, my best friend and fellow other bridesmaid, shouts from the other side of the pedal tavern. "I still have to find me a cowboy!"

I don't bother telling her that the only cowboys in Nashville are wanna-be country singers and guys who bought boots for the weekend from Wal-Mart.

"Screw the cowboys. I want to find me one of those football players Whitley knows."

The slurred comment comes from Emmilene, Ella Mae's sister, and, much to all of our dismay, maid of honor. The bridal party consists of me, Betsy, and two of our other sorority sisters from Alabama; her high school best friend; and, of course, Emmilene.

Ella Mae let her pick out the color of the dresses. It is horrible.

She let her decide on the theme for the bridal shower. She went with an Old Southern Tea Party. Ella Mae hated it, but didn't say a word. She's too nice and too meek to speak up.

The only thing she has gotten right so far is the bachelorette party in Nashville. And let's be real, the only reason this isn't a disaster is because it's pretty hard to screw this up.

Though if anyone could, it would be Emmilene.

"Like I told you earlier, I don't know them," I say. I wasn't going to answer her, but she's staring at me like I'm supposed to make a Nashville Fury player pop up out of nowhere. "My brother is the coach. I don't know any of the players."

"Yeah right," she says, tossing back a piece of her red hair that is blowing in the wind. "You just want them all for yourself."

Now I ignore her because I don't want to start anything with a drunk Emmilene. She's nasty enough when she's sober, and we have a long night ahead of us.

I wasn't lying when I said I don't know any of the Nashville Fury players, despite my brother being the head coach. Yes, I come to his home games. Yes, I have met a few players in passing.

The truth is, they don't do it for me. And not just them—

football players in general. Or football fans. Alabama fans, to be specific. When you are from Birmingham, you can't go ten feet without someone yelling "Roll Tide!"

I don't have anything against the sport. I love football. You can't grow up in the McAvoy house and not live for Saturdays and Sundays in the fall. I can probably out talk most men when it comes to football, though they doubt that a former beauty queen knows the difference between a touchdown and an illegal block in the back.

The problem is that once football players, or fans, realize who I am—the daughter and sister of Crimson Tide football royalty—they stop seeing me as a woman and start seeing me as a ticket.

My dad was the best quarterback to ever play at Alabama and is a hall of fame player as a professional. My brother, also an Alabama great, is the hottest coach in professional football and happens to be the head football coach in the town I'm currently visiting.

Then there is me. Only in my family does being named Miss Teen Alabama and running my own company at age twenty-six come in a distant third on the list of family accomplishments.

That's why I'll pass on football players. And Crimson Tide fans.

So, basically, every straight man in the state of Alabama.

"Oh, come on, Whit," Betsy says, swaying a bit as I'm guessing she's starting to feel the copious amount of shots we have taken today. "You can't call up a few players? Or maybe your brother. He's hot as fuck."

I cringe at her words. "Don't ever say that again."

"I mean, look at him!" she says, pointing to a billboard with Hunter's face plastered on it. "No one should be that good-looking."

"You know he's engaged, right?" I ask. "And I happen to very much like his fiancée."

She just shrugs. "Whatever. Nothing is final until a preacher says so."

I just shake my head because that's all I can do. Everyone has that one friend with questionable morals. Betsy is that friend for me.

"If I can't bang your brother, maybe we'll find some other guys tonight. What happens in Nashville stays in Nashville!"

This causes the rest of the bachelorette party to raise their glasses and give another "woo." Except for me.

"I don't think that's how the saying goes," I say, though I can't help but laugh at Betsy's enthusiasm.

"Oh, come on, Whitley. We're in a new city for the weekend. Why not have some fun? And if that fun happens to be of the naked variety, so be it."

I take another drink and let Betsy's words sink in. I'm not normally a one-night stand kind of girl, but that's because of who I am. In Birmingham, it's hard for me to go anywhere without people knowing who I am, or who my family is. Besides being a McAvoy, I'm one of the most successful fundraising consultants in Birmingham. If you want to raise money for your foundation, you call me. I get it done.

So, I try to date, though it's normally unsuccessful. I don't hook up. Frankly, my love life is quite pathetic.

Maybe Betsy is right. Maybe this is my weekend to have some fun. Let my hair down. Live a little on the wild side.

Because in this city, I'm not Hunter's sister, Bo's daughter or the girl hired to raise millions for your foundation.

I'm just Whitley McAvoy.

And that sounds just fine by me.

2

JAKE

"I DARE YOU."

I shoot a look to Trent, making sure I heard him correctly.

"You what?"

"You heard me," he says, though, in all honesty, I don't know if I did hear him. We're in the middle of a downtown Nashville bar on a Saturday night in June. I can barely hear myself think.

"Let's pretend I didn't," I say, taking another swig of my beer. Because if he did say what I think he said, I'm going to need the backing of some liquid encouragement.

"I said," he begins, looking over to the bachelorette party, then looking back at me, "I dare you to go over to that bride and show her Officer Sexy."

Nope. He said exactly what I thought he said. Though I have no clue why one of my buddies is daring me to give a lap dance to a woman I've never met.

Actually, I do know why. It's Trent. Trent is "that guy" of our friend group. He's the guy who talks the biggest but has zero game. He's the one to come up with the shenanigan but will never go through with it. If I had to guess, he noticed one of the women in the group, likely a redhead, and he wants to talk to her, but he won't make the first move. Therefore, he needs me to break the ice. With a lap dance.

That and he wants the chance to get Officer Sexy on video. He's still pissed he missed it the one and only time it has happened.

"What's going on?" Knox says, reappearing from lord knows where with a girl on his arm.

"I dared Jake to go show that bride over there that Officer Sexy is in the house," Trent says, tilting his head toward the group of women.

"Can't you just go over and talk to whoever you want to?" Knox asks, confirming my theory. "One of these days, we aren't going to be around to get women for you."

"What?" Trent says, acting shocked at the accusation. "That's not it at all. Though that redhead is pretty cute. I just think it's been a while since Officer Sexy has made an appearance and it's due time to break him out. What better way than for an about-to-be-bride?"

I roll my eyes at the nickname, and now I really don't want to take the dare. I'm not in the mood. Hell, I wasn't even in the mood to come to Nashville tonight. I would have been just as happy grabbing a beer at The Joint, the only bar in Rolling Hills, our hometown about an hour south of Nashville.

But Trent whined so much, Knox and I finally gave in. Though by the way this girl is latching onto Knox, I doubt he's complaining much.

"Yeah, Officer Sexy," Knox says, egging me on. "Go show them how you earned the name."

"It's bad enough when he says it," I say, shooting a thumb in Trent's direction. "When you say it… well, it's downright dirty."

"Yeah it is," Knox says, wagging his eyebrows. "Or should I say dirty dancing?"

Sometimes I regret learning to do the worm for the fifth-grade talent show. Or maybe it was taking dance lessons in seventh grade to impress Missy Fischer. Either way, those two events had a major impact on the fact that I'm now in a Nashville honkytonk seriously contemplating giving a woman I don't know a lap dance.

That and I've never been shy. Trent was the smart one. Knox was the athlete.

Me? I was the outgoing one.

And I never turn down a dare.

Never.

That is how Officer Sexy started in the first place. A dare.

I picked up an overtime shift one night, and I got a call that there was a disturbance at The Joint. Being the dutiful police officer I am, I hightailed it over to the bar. Only when I walked in, I didn't find a fight—I found Daisy and Doris Abernathy each sitting on chairs with balloons tied to the back of them. I learned when I arrived that it was their ninety-fifth birthday party, and all they asked for was a dance from their favorite Rolling Hills police officer.

I wasn't going to do it. I'm a respected police officer and member of the community. I speak every year at career day, coach Little League and make sure I volunteer each year at the annual summer festival.

Then I heard the three words I've never been able to resist.

"I dare you."

They came from Porter, the owner of The Joint. I've taken one too many dares at his bar to know those words are my kryptonite. Next thing I know, I'm giving the town's twin spinsters a birthday present they'll never forget.

And neither will I. They might be ninety-five, but they were... we'll call them handsy.

Little did I know the pictures and video from that night would live in Rolling Hills history and the name Officer Sexy would be born.

I haven't been able to live it down since.

"Come on, Evans," Trent says, trying to egg me on. "Just look at her. You going to leave a bride hanging?"

I take a look over to the bachelorette party, but it's not the bride who catches my attention. Standing next to her is the most beautiful woman I have ever seen in my life.

She is laughing at something, and her smile is lighting up this entire bar. Her blond hair is styled on top of her head, but I can tell it's long enough that it would flow past her shoulders if she let it down.

With her bare shoulders on display, all I want to do is place my lips there to see what she would taste like.

She's gorgeous. Stunning. Unlike any woman I have ever seen in my life. Granted, the dating scene in Rolling Hills is limited due to the fact that we have all known each other since we were kids.

But it doesn't matter if we are in Nashville, Rolling Hills, or in the middle of Times Square; she would still be the most beautiful woman in the room. No question about it.

And I need to know who she is.

"Dare accepted," I say, taking one last pull of my beer. "Go to the jukebox. Find the song."

3

WHITLEY

"LET'S LEAVE, THIS PLACE SUCKS!"

Of course, the displeasure is coming from Emmilene. I want to tell her that this bar was her idea, but I don't. I didn't wake up today choosing violence.

"I like it," Ella Mae says, taking a sip of her drink. "Plus, I lovvvvvvve this bushwacker!"

I can't help but laugh at a drunk Ella Mae as Emmilene lets out a huff and plops down on a barstool. Yes, I know it's not very nice that I'm secretly loving the fact that the wicked sister is having a miserable time. My southern passive-aggressive mean streak is reveling in this.

"What's with her?" Betsy asks, coming back from the dance floor to stand next to me. "Wait... let me guess. She just realized that the stick is so far up her ass she'll never be able to get it out?"

I can't help but laugh. "I don't think so yet. I'm not going to be the one to tell her."

"Neither am I. That would require conversation. And I'd rather go celibate then engage in conversation with the evil sister."

I lift my glass to hers. "I'll drink to that."

Betsy leans into the bar to order a drink, and I take the minute to people watch. I love people watching, especially in a new city. Birmingham might be a big city for Alabama, but I feel like I've been seeing the same people everywhere I go. Or maybe it's because people seem to know me wherever I go.

And that can get stifling.

I want to meet someone new. Someone like I've never met before—someone who doesn't want me to get them an autograph.

"Pardon me, I couldn't help but notice that one of you lovely ladies is getting married soon?"

Some women have a thing for arms. Some go for abs or a smile. Me? Give me a man with a deep voice that I just know would say filthy things to me behind closed doors, and I am a pile of mush.

This man, who I've not yet made eye contact with? This voice coming from behind me? I don't even need to look at him to know that he would leave me satisfied in all the right ways. Add in his country twang, and I'm already melting.

"That's me!" Ella Mae squeals, raising her hand like she's in grade school.

The mystery man laughs, and shit, his laugh is just as deep and sexy as his voice.

I want to turn around and get a look at him. But I'm afraid if I do, it will ruin the mental picture I have quickly conjured. In my mind, he's a bit rugged. He's wearing those country-boy jeans that fit in all the right places and leave nothing to the imagination. And he's wearing a cowboy hat. A real one. Not one you can buy at the souvenir shop at the airport.

And plaid. He's definitely wearing a plaid shirt. I bet his sleeves are rolled up, showing off his forearms.

Okay, so maybe I have a thing for arms, too.

"Well then, darlin', what kind of gentleman would I be if I didn't offer to buy you and your friends a drink?"

"I'll take a drink!" Emmilene yells from the other side of Ella Mae. I quickly look over at her and realize that she's staring at this man like he's dinner, and she hasn't eaten in days.

That's all the cue I need to turn around and finally put a face to the image I've concocted in my head.

Sweet baby Jesus.

He's… I don't even have words. And I'm never speechless.

Though I have a feeling if this man were to get me naked, he'd be leaving me speechless for a whole different reason.

He's what a man should look like. In every definition of that phrase.

I was mostly right about the choice of clothes. I hit the nail on the head with the plaid and jeans. Instead of the cowboy hat, he has opted for a backward trucker cap. Usually, I'm not a fan of that look. But on this guy? I'm a fan.

A big, big fan.

Then there are the things I didn't imagine about him, but I don't even know if I could have if I tried.

The skin I can see is bronzed only the way it can be from working outside in the southern sun. His muscles fill out his shirt just right to pull at the fabric, but not too much where it might rip. His smile is that fine line between cocky and confident and shows off a dimple in his left cheek.

Then there are his eyes. They are the color of my favorite milk chocolate.

And they are currently burning into me right now.

"And what about you, sweetness?" he asks, his voice softening a bit, though the look in his eyes is more intense. "What can I get you? You look a little thirsty."

You.

I almost said it. It was on the tip of my tongue because that's literally the only word I can think of.

But I don't have a chance to answer. Just as who knows what word is about to come out of my mouth, the unmistakable first beat of the song "Pony" comes blaring through the jukebox. The song might be as old as I am, but that doesn't mean I don't know it.

And apparently, so does Sexy Plaid Cowboy Man.

He reaches for Ella Mae's hand, his hips slowly starting to move in beat with the music, and when I turn to look at my best friend, her face is twenty different shades of red. I don't know if this man realizes that he just picked the shyest bachelorette in the history of bachelorettes to try and give an impromptu lap dance.

"What's a bachelorette party without a dance?" he asks, bringing her out of her chair. "Don't worry, I don't bite."

"I… no… I can't!" she squeals, immediately turning toward me. "Here! Dance with Whitley!"

"What?" I let out, not having a second to take in what's happening before Ella Mae grabs my hand, yanks me off my stool, and slingshots me into the hardest chest I've ever felt.

I look up to see his brown eyes taking me in, and that cocky smile is back with full force.

"Your friend doesn't want a dance?" he says, his voice hitting me even harder this close to him.

"She's shy," I say, trying not to melt from the sound of his deep timbre.

"Are you?" he asks, a hint of mischief playing on his face.

I don't break eye contact, though I can see Emmilene out of the corner of my eye, her mouth wide open as she can't believe what is happening.

Oh, this just got so much better.

"Absolutely not. What do you got, cowboy?"

4

JAKE

HER WORDS ARE a straight shot of adrenaline through my body.

I might not be a cowboy, but I wouldn't mind giving her the ride of her life.

When I took the dare, I figured I'd give the bride a dance—it is her last hurrah as a single woman. She should have at least one crazy story from her bachelorette party. What's crazier than a lap dance from a random stranger? I figured that would give me an ice breaker into the group. Hopefully, the blonde beauty would be impressed by my moves and we could strike up a conversation after. I'd buy her a drink. And maybe if I was lucky, I could give her a dance of her own.

In private.

Like he's reading my mind, I see Knox bring me a chair, placing it behind me. Where he got it, I have no clue, but I'm not about to look a gift horse in the mouth.

"You ready?" I ask, spinning her around to place her on the chair. She doesn't take her eyes off me as she slowly lowers herself, and fuck if that doesn't spur me on even more.

"Let's see what you got."

This is now so much more than a stupid dare from Trent. I have one shot to make me unforgettable to this woman, and I sure as hell am not about to blow it.

I turn my back, taking a few steps away from her chair. As soon as the words of the chorus drop, I pivot around, taking one step before I slide toward her, landing right at her knees, which I promptly push apart. I take a quick glance up at her eyes, and my movement has its desired effect.

She's turned on. Her jaw is open slightly and her cheeks are flushed.

Perfect.

I push myself up, snaking my body between her spread legs as I feel the hat come off my head. It's only when she slips it on hers do I realize she's the thief.

Oh, she's going to pay for that.

I smirk before stepping over her legs, bringing them back together as I straddle her on the chair. My hips begin to roll back and forth, grazing her lap every time they pass each other, my hands gripping the back of her chair. I can't help but see more than a few cameras are capturing this. I know for a fact Trent is one of them. I don't give a shit right now. All that is on my mind is making sure this woman never forgets this.

I lean back a little, taking in her face when I see the smile that attracted me to her just minutes ago.

"That all you got?" she asks, challenge laced in her words.

"What do you think?"

"I think you're holding back."

The challenge in her eyes and the teasing in her voice go straight to my dick, and I have to shift my movement so she doesn't see what she is doing to me.

I take a step back, so I'm no longer straddling her, but continue to move to the beat as I walk behind her. I place my hands on her shoulders, hoping it gives me a few seconds to calm my dick down. It's no use. The softness of her skin against my rough hands feels way too fucking good. Instead of calming myself down, all it does is ramp me up, and the next thing I know, I'm spinning from behind the chair, landing right back in front of her.

I don't know what it is about me and dancing, but it's just something that has come naturally to me. I know that's not normal for men, but for me, it is. Even though the dance lessons only lasted a few years, whenever I hear a song and feel the beat, my body takes over.

Right now, it has a mind of its own.

I roll my body, bringing my shirt up slightly to give her a tease, but not enough to get me kicked out of the bar. I take another step closer to her, letting my hips gyrate against her as I lean into her ear.

"You ready?" I ask.

I feel her shiver when my breath hits her neck. "For what?"

"You'll see."

I push away from her, take a few steps to turn away before dropping down and doing a backward roll, pushing myself up just slightly to sit perfectly in her lap. My dick is against her center, and my ass is against her stomach as I start basically dry humping her on this chair, my hands on the floor the only thing holding me up.

"Sweet Jesus…"

She doesn't say the words loudly, but somehow, I hear them over the roar of the crowd, which is currently going wild at moves you can usually only see in Vegas. The applause only gets louder as the song comes to a close. While I'm upset it's done—I still had a few more moves up my sleeve—I'm also glad it is.

I need to see her. I need to hear that sweet voice again. I need to see if she enjoyed the show.

I need to know her name.

I right myself and quickly turn to her. She's still sitting in the chair, and the look on her face is exactly what I wanted to see.

Her eyes are heated. Her cheeks are flushed. Her breathing is heavy.

Best. Dare. Ever.

I take a step forward and hold my hand out to her, which she immediately takes.

"What did you think?" I ask as she stands up.

"I'm not sure," she says, that playful smile coming back on her face. "I've seen better."

I put a hand to my heart, feigning shock. "And where, may I ask, have you seen better moves than those before?"

"You're good, don't get me wrong," she says, taking a few steps toward the bar, though not letting go of my hand. "But Channing Tatum might want his moves back."

I laugh. "Movies and Vegas review shows don't count."

"Oh," she says, putting her manicured finger to her lips as she pretends to think. "Then I am wrong. You win, sir. Best real life lap dance I've ever had."

"Damn straight," I say, ordering myself a beer and telling the bartender to get her whatever she'd like. "And you didn't even get to see my good moves."

She turns to me, her eyebrows shooting up in question. "Those weren't your good moves? I thought I told you not to hold back."

I smile, leaning in a little closer. "My good moves are saved for a more… private audience."

I feel her shiver again, loving the fact that I have this effect on her. Lord knows, she has the same effect on me.

"That audience must be real lucky," she says, reaching for the water she ordered from the bartender. "You've got some moves… oh my gosh, I don't even know your name!"

I laugh as a look of mortification rolls through her face. "I don't know yours either, sweetness. So, it makes us even. I'm Jake."

"You don't know mine?"

That wasn't what I was expecting.

"Should I?"

"Whitley!" someone yells, and Whitley looks over her shoulder. "We are getting ready to head to the next bar. Are you coming or are you going to keep flirting with Wish.com Magic Mike?"

I would laugh at the joke, except the jealousy is rolling off of the girl's tongue. Frankly, it's not very attractive.

"Oh, come on, darling. I'm at least the Wal-Mart version."

She lets out a huff as she storms off. I look back at Whitley, and all I see is sadness in her eyes.

And that just won't do.

"I should go," she says, gesturing to her group. "It's my best friend's bachelorette party and her bitchy sister will never let me live it down if I ditch them for you."

I smile, giving her hand a squeeze. "We can't have that."

"I guess this is goodbye?"

"Oh no, sweetness," I say, quickly pulling out my wallet and tossing a few twenties on the bar to cover my tab. "This party is just getting started."

5

WHITLEY

"SEE, I think you're lying. You are a cowboy, aren't you?"

Jake smiles at my joke as he climbs up from the ring where he just finished riding the mechanical bull—for an impressive thirty-five seconds.

"I don't lie," he says, wrapping his arms around my waist. "While yes, I am a cop and not a cowboy, that doesn't mean I can't ride."

His eyebrows start wagging up and down, and I can't help but laugh at his playfulness. Since we left the bar that will forever in my memory be known as "the place where I got a lap dance from a complete stranger," Jake hasn't left my side.

And I don't want him to.

We've laughed. We've done shots. We've gotten to know each other, even if it is just the basics. He came clean that no, he's not a cowboy. That was after I dared him to go on the mechanical bull. I also learned from his friend, Knox, that he doesn't turn down dares, including the one tonight that led to my lap dance.

Luckily, we've kept the conversation light and pretty superficial. I haven't had to tell him my last name, therefore avoiding the chance that he could look at me differently once that information is public.

Because I don't want him looking at me differently than he is right now—like I'm the only woman in this bar. I'm sure the girls, specifically Emmilene, would be giving me shit about it, but his friends have been keeping them company all night. Especially the one Jake introduced as Trent. It seems that crazy-bitchy redheads are his cup of tea.

"Where did you learn to ride?" I ask, loving the little bit I've gotten to know about him tonight.

"I'm from a small town about an hour south of here. You don't grow up in Rolling Hills and not learn to ride a horse," he says, taking a seat on the barstool, pulling me in so I'm standing between his legs. "What about you? Where are you from?"

I take a second to wrap my arms around his neck, hoping I can be honest and not give too much away. "Birmingham. Born and raised. We're only here for the weekend."

"As so many are," he says, pulling me in a little tighter. "I take it in Birmingham you don't ride horses?"

"Some do, but not me," I say, hoping to steer the conversation. "I must ask. Where did you learn to dance like that?"

The question has been on my mind all night. Either the guy used to be a dancer in Vegas or he is the best-kept secret for bachelorette parties in the state of Tennessee.

"I can't be telling you all my secrets," he says, his dimple popping up as he gives me a small smile. "Not even Knox knows that, and he's been my best friend since we were in diapers."

"Now I'm even more curious," I say, letting my fingers play at the nape of his neck.

He looks up and takes a breath before meeting my gaze again. "If I tell you, I'm going to need a big secret from you."

Shit. My big secret is that my brother is one of the most popular men in this town, and he most likely has seen highlights of my daddy playing football. But if I say no, he'll wonder what I'm hiding.

And for some reason, I don't want to hide things from this man. I might not want to tell him the big one yet, but that doesn't mean I want this conversation, or night, to end.

"Let's see what you got, first," I say, hoping my answer doesn't come off as suspicious.

"You drive a hard bargain, sweetness," he says, brushing a loose piece of hair away from my face. "But since you asked so nicely, I guess I can tell you."

"I'm flattered."

He looks around, and if I had to guess, it's to make sure Knox or Trent aren't within earshot. "When I was in middle school, I took dance lessons to impress a girl. Obviously, I didn't learn the moves I used on you tonight in Miss Margie's hip hop class, but it taught me the basics. I guess I just picked up some things over the years."

My eyes grow wide. "You were willing to take dance lessons to impress a girl?"

He laughs, pulling me closer. "Out of that whole admission, that's what you took away from it?"

"Only because that is the sweetest thing I've ever heard. Did you get her?"

He shakes his head. "Nope. Turns out she had a thing for Knox the whole time. Not even the worm was enough to impress her."

"Aw, poor baby," I say, and without thinking about it, I lean in and kiss his lips.

I didn't even mean to. The reaction was instantaneous, and I couldn't stop myself.

Though judging by the fact that Jake's hands are now cupping my cheeks, deepening the kiss, I don't think he's mad about it.

His tongue gently licks across my closed lips, asking for

entry. I've never made out with someone in public before. The fear of pictures, or the incident getting back to my parents or clients, is enough of a deterrent for me.

But this kiss? I don't care if the *National Enquirer* or *TMZ* is here taking photos, I never want this kiss to end.

His lips are smooth, despite the rest of him being so hard. Even though this kiss is a byproduct of a fast and crazy night, the kiss isn't rushed or hurried. It's like we are both savoring it. Like neither of us wants it to end.

"Get a room, you two!"

Betsy's voice breaks our moment and our lips part, though neither of us moves very far. I should feel embarrassed—I just kissed a guy at a bar who I met four hours ago when he gave me a lap dance. But I don't.

Actually, I want to keep kissing him.

And maybe even more.

"Should we?" I ask, feeling bolder than I ever have in my life. I've never had a one-night stand, let alone initiated one.

"Should we what?"

I take a breath, hoping I'm feeling the same thing he is. "Should we get a room?"

He smiles, placing another kiss on my lips. "That's the best idea I've heard in a long time."

———

I HAVE NEVER BEEN SO excited to have booked a room by myself this weekend.

I'm also giving myself a mental pat on the back for wearing a tube top. It's giving Jake plenty of room to kiss as I stand outside my hotel door, doing my best to try and get this damn hotel card to swipe.

"You have to do it gently," he says between kisses.

As soon as he puts his lips back on my skin, I melt into him. His arms are snaked around my waist, and they are the only thing holding me up as I get lost in the feeling of his mouth on me.

"Mmm," I purr, almost forgetting about what I was trying to do just seconds before.

"You know, I can kiss a lot more of you if we're in your room."

His words spur me back into action, and with one swipe of the card, the green light flashes, allowing us entry into my room.

I push the door open, almost stumbling over the entryway because Jake refuses to take his lips off of me. Not that I'm complaining. Jake's mouth on me is like nothing I've ever felt before.

I haven't been with a ton of men, but I wouldn't call me inexperienced, either. But this? I didn't know just kisses to the neck could induce such want. Need. Like if I don't have him in the next ten seconds, I'll combust.

Which only makes me wonder what it would feel like for his mouth to be on other parts of me.

"Bed. Now."

His deep voice hits me just like I thought it would when I first heard it a few hours ago. But now that we're here? It's all that much more potent.

"What do you have in mind?" I ask, sitting on the bed, letting my fingers travel underneath his shirt. His skin is hot and hard, just like I knew it would be.

"Oh, sweetness, do you really want to know?" he says, beginning to undo the buttons of his shirt.

I can't take my eyes off of him as he slowly undresses in front of me. With each button that pops open, another part of his fabulous chest is revealed. His muscles are lean and defined. Not overly bulky, but perfectly sculpted for his frame.

And all I want to do is hold on to those biceps as he does whatever he wants to do with me.

"I do," I say, slowly moving back on the bed.

"First," he says as he starts to climb onto the bed, slowly placing his body on top of me. "There is a lot more of you that I haven't gotten to kiss yet."

"What are you waiting for then?" I ask, hoping my voice doesn't sound as desperate as I am to have his mouth back on me.

He doesn't move; instead, his eyes are looking into me even deeper than they were before. "You're okay, right?"

I cock my head, confused by his question. "Of course, I am. Why?"

He lets out a breath as he sweeps back a piece of hair off my forehead. "Tonight was insane. Amazing, but insane. I just want to make sure this is what you want."

I'm flattered and frustrated all at the same time. On the one hand, how sweet is it that this man is making sure that I'm okay with whatever is about to happen?

On the other, can't he tell by the way that my hips keep seeking his that I needed this ten minutes ago?

"While I think that you making sure I'm good is the sweetest thing I've ever heard," I say, letting my hands start to trace the ridges of his abs. "If you don't kiss me again in five seconds I—"

I don't even get to finish my sentence as his lips come crashing onto mine. There is nothing soft about this kiss. This kiss is hard and rough and everything I need.

I've never been kissed like this. The men I've kissed before now seem hesitant and inexperienced. This kiss is all-consuming. I'm feeling this in every cell of my body. This kiss is the one they talk about in songs that make you question every other kiss you've had before and wonder if you'll ever be kissed like this again.

His hands begin to explore, traveling up my top and

quickly bringing it over my head. The strapless bra I'm wearing all of a sudden feels stifling. Thank goodness he removes it swiftly, his mouth quickly finding his way to my breasts.

"Oh my God," I say, though it probably comes out more like one word. Or maybe it's incoherent syllables? I honestly don't care, and by the way Jake is taking turns nipping and sucking on each nipple, I don't think he does either.

Can someone have an orgasm this way? I think I read one time about nipple play, but I thought that was a myth. To be honest, I sometimes think that orgasms themselves are myths. I think I've had one. Once. But then again, that guy did need my help to finish me, so I don't know if that counts.

Jake's mouth continues to take what he wants as his hands slide down my sides, around to my front to undo the button of my shorts. I'm ready to kick them off to help him out, but I can't. The feeling of him paralyzes my body—first, my breasts, then my stomach. And just as I think that's where he's going to stay for a minute, he pulls down my shorts and thong in one swoop, and his mouth is on my center.

Holy.

Shit.

My hips immediately buck, the sensation of his tongue against my opening too much to handle. His hands immediately move to my hip bones, holding me down so he can take what he wants.

"I knew you'd be sweet," he says, his voice another octave lower. Holy hell, is his sex voice hot. "Now lie back and let me taste you."

My goodness, this man is going to ruin me. If his tongue was doing wicked things to me when we were kissing, then what he is doing now is downright evil. His tongue is flicking rapidly on my clit as he puts one, then two, fingers inside me, driving me insane from the inside out.

Even if this is as far as we go tonight, Jake, the dancing police officer, will have forever ruined me in the oral sex department.

"Jake!" I scream, the beginning of an orgasm beginning to take over me. Which also makes me know for a fact that I have never had one. Because this is unlike anything I have ever felt.

"That's right, sweetness, come all over me."

His words are dirty and deep, and I love every minute of it. It's like they have a direct line to my core because, in seconds, I'm exploding all over him. His fingers slowly bring me down, though I doubt I'll be able to control my breathing anytime soon.

I should be embarrassed. I have never done that before. I almost don't want to look Jake in the eye, but I feel his gaze burning into me, and I can't help but look up at him as he hovers over my body.

His eyes are just as heated as mine.

"That was…" I can't finish the sentence, the aftershocks of my orgasms still running through me.

"Not the end," he says, finishing my sentence. It wasn't what I was about to say, but I'm not about to argue with him.

He places a kiss on my forehead before standing up. Holy crap, how did I forget that he's not naked yet? That is just a travesty.

His eyes don't leave mine as he undoes his belt, takes his wallet out of his back pocket to grab a condom, and quickly pushes his jeans down. His hard cock is pushing against his gray boxer briefs, begging to be released.

"I wish I could take this slow," he says, beginning to rub himself over the top of his briefs. God, that is so sexy. "But I don't know if I can."

"Who said I wanted it slow?"

I don't know where this bold seductress is coming from. Apparently, she also suggests leaving a bar with a man she just met and challenges him during a lap dance.

But I like her. And by the look in Jake's eye, he likes her too.

Without taking his eyes off me, Jake sheds his boxers, rolls on the condom, then grabs my ankles, pulling me toward him to the end of the bed. I shriek in surprise but am quickly quieted as Jake fills me to the hilt, keeping his promise that this wasn't going to be slow and easy.

His cock is long and thick and… oh my God, I don't know what it just did there, but it hit a spot inside me I didn't know existed.

"More. Jake, I want more."

Do I want more? Apparently, I do if that's what I said. Then again, I've never been fucked like this in my life. It's hard and intense and consuming and amazing.

"You want more, sweetness? You sure you can handle that?"

His deep voice combined with his Tennessee twang does something right there to me, and I know that even if this is the only time we do this, I'm never going to forget this night as long as I live.

"Don't hold back on me, cowboy."

And he doesn't. The man starts driving into me like he's trying to brand himself into my body. It's fast. It's furious. It's a little rough.

It's everything I never knew I wanted.

"Ah! Jake!"

I'm pretty sure the whole hotel heard me scream, but I don't care. My orgasm rips through me as Jake follows soon after.

Yup. No matter what happens. I'm never going to forget this night.

Not as long as I'm breathing on this earth.

6

JAKE

I DON'T REMEMBER the last time I didn't wake up to an alarm. Though, I must say, waking up to Whitley rubbing her ass against my dick is the best wake-up call I've ever gotten.

"Good morning, cowboy," she says, her voice raspy and barely awake. I bring her in closer to me, wondering when she scooted away from my embrace.

Yes, I'm the guy who likes to cuddle when he sleeps. If Knox or Trent ever find out about this, I'll never live it down. Officer Sexy is bad enough. I have a feeling my house would be filled with stuffed animals if this knowledge ever made it to them.

But you go to sleep naked next to a woman like Whitley and tell me you wouldn't try to keep her as close as possible. Holding her in my arms last night after we drifted off after a second round is a feeling I've never felt before. Though at the time, I chalked some of that up to the remaining booze and adrenaline of the night.

But now, lying here, in the Nashville morning light, I'm getting the same feeling. And I have no idea what to make of it.

I've had girlfriends, though none have ever been serious. I

never thought about staying in bed with them all day, just so I could hold them for five more minutes.

I place my lips on the back of her neck, loving the way it physically sends shivers down her whole body. "Good morning, sweetness."

Neither of us says anything for a minute, and I know for me, I'm trying my all not to think about what happens when we leave this bed. Right now, we're in a bubble. Nothing can touch us. The outside world, specifically the distance between us, doesn't exist.

Right now, we're just two people lying naked together in bed. But as soon as one of us moves, the spell will be broken.

"I don't want to move," she says in almost a whisper.

"I feel the same way."

"Do we have to?"

I laugh, loving that our minds are thinking the same thing. "I guess it depends on how long you have this room for. Though that can be fixed with one phone call to the front desk."

She turns over to face me, and I adjust my arms so I don't have to let go of her. "I hate that I have to go back to Birmingham today."

She doesn't make eye contact with me when she says it. But I can hear the sadness in her voice, and it just about guts me. Nope, that will not do.

"Come here," I say, grabbing her by the hips and picking her up so she's now straddling me.

"What are you doing?" she says, her voice already lighter.

"There will be no sadness here," I say, lacing her fingers through mine. "There's no reason to be."

"But there is." She starts tracing my chest with her fingers. Damn, that feels good. "You… me… and… Last night was…"

"Awesome? Fantastic? Five stars, would recommend doing again?"

This makes her smile. "I was thinking more like amazing."

"I'm good with amazing."

"That's the problem. It was amazing, which makes me sad that we had this great night and now... now we have to say goodbye."

The sound of that silence is the bubble bursting.

I want to tell her that it doesn't have to be goodbye. Birmingham is only two hours from Rolling Hills. We could see each other. Maybe I'd come down on weekends, or she could come to see me.

But does she want that? If she's already thinking that this is it, I doubt she'd want to try a long-distance thing. Especially with a man she's known less than a day. She was direct with me last night. If she wants this, she'll say so, right?

Then there are the obvious differences between us. I'm a cop in a three-stoplight town. She's a city girl who has probably never heard of Rolling Hills. No. This needs to end on a good note. For both of us. I don't want to remember the sadness in her voice right now. I want to remember the smile that made me stop dead in my tracks.

"I don't like goodbyes. Or sad things," I begin, sitting up with her still straddling me. If this is going to be the last time I get to hold her, I need to feel as much of her against me as possible. "We are going to remember this night for what it was. A crazy night that led to two people sharing something neither of us will forget. A night where two people laughed and had fun and made a memory that will be hard to ever replace. How can that be sad?"

She takes in a deep breath, lacing her hands behind my neck. "You're right. We had a great night. Nothing sad about it."

"Exactly," I say, leaning in to kiss her, which she returns eagerly. This is our last kiss. I need to make it a good one.

And I need to memorize it. Memorize her. I need to never forget the way her tongue feels against mine. The way her lips, even in the morning, are the softest things I've ever felt. The way she gives my bottom lip a little nibble when she wants me to go deeper.

I could kiss this girl forever. And I fucking hate the fact that I'm not going to get to.

The sound of her cell phone startles us, breaking the moment. Probably a good thing. God knows, I wasn't going to end it anytime soon.

The phone keeps ringing, but she doesn't make a move to go get it. Instead, she sits on my lap, our foreheads touching.

"I will never forget you, sweetness," I say, placing one last kiss on her forehead.

"You better not, cowboy. You better not."

7

JAKE

"EIGHT BALL, CORNER POCKET."

I hear the words come out of Knox's mouth, but I don't even bother to look as he takes his shot. I know it's going to go in. He's made every shot tonight.

I haven't made one.

"Man, you are worse than usual. Grumpier too," he says, walking over and grabbing his beer. "What crawled up your ass tonight?"

"No clue, man. Want to go again?" I say, quickly making my way to put another dollar of quarters into the pool table at The Joint.

"I mean, if you want to get your ass kicked again, I'm happy to do it."

Normally, playing pool at The Joint on a Saturday night is my way of de-stressing from the week. Usually, my week consists of forty hours of work, a few hours at the gym each night, and helping my mom tackle the never-ending list of problems around her house.

But this week was different. This week I was plagued by

thoughts of a certain blonde-haired beauty who has taken up permanent residence in my brain.

Especially tonight, when just this time last week, I was giving her a dance I'll never forget. It's almost funny if you think about it. Who knew a stupid dare from Trent would have the outcome it did?

"What are you laughing at?" Knox asks, walking back toward the pool table. "And if you say nothin', I'm going to call Daisy and Doris and tell them you want to give them an encore."

That gets my attention. "You wouldn't dare."

Knox raises his eyebrows, almost challenging me to call his bluff.

"Fine. But you play dirty."

He laughs. "Never claimed otherwise."

I take a seat back at our table as Knox lines up his shot.

"So, remember that girl from last week?"

Knox pulls the stick back and pushes it forward, dispensing the balls around the table. This might be the first shot he's taken tonight that a ball didn't go in. "The one that you dry humped in the middle of the bar then left with later? The reason I had to drive back to Nashville on a Sunday morning to pick your ass up? Vaguely."

I punch his arm as we switch spots. "Yeah, her. I've just been thinking about her, that's all. No big deal."

No shock, I miss my shot, and Knox steps back up, quickly draining his first attempt. "No big deal, my ass. You've been either pissed off or mopey all week."

"Have not."

"You have. And luckily for you, I have a brilliant idea that could make you less of an asshole."

I almost don't want to ask. "And what would that be, oh wise one?"

He sinks another shot before looking in my direction. "You could, I don't know, call her."

I let out a sigh as he lines up his next shot. "We didn't exchange numbers. I don't even know her last name."

My admission makes Knox whiff on his shot. "You didn't do what? Dude, you were into her. And unless I all of a sudden can't read women, she was all about you. So, why the fuck wouldn't you exchange numbers!"

I shrug my shoulders. "We just didn't. We both decided it was for the best."

"That is the damn stupidest thing you've ever done. And I know all of the stupid shit you've done. Now I don't feel bad for you."

Was it stupid? Maybe. At the time, it felt right. But now? Maybe not so much. I thought this feeling would go away by now, but it's only getting worse.

"Thanks for the invite assholes."

Trent's voice snaps me out of the thoughts that usually send me going down the Whitley what-if rabbit hole.

"We did invite you, asshole. Check your messages."

Trent gives Knox a questioning look as he pulls out his phone, hopefully checking his text messages where he will find a message in our group text saying to meet at The Joint. I was actually shocked he wasn't here when I arrived. Trent never passes on a night out.

"Excuse me for missing it," he says, taking a seat at the table that is currently housing the bucket of beers Knox and I split. "Must be because I'm getting so many notifications on the other apps on my phone I can't keep them straight."

Knox and I look at each other, both clearly confused as to what the fuck he's talking about.

"All right, I'll bite," I say, knowing that if I don't, he's just going to tell us anyway. "What is blowing up your phone so much that you missed the invite."

"I'm so glad it was you who asked, Officer Sexy."

That gets my attention. I kind of hoped that Officer Sexy

would die a slow death in Nashville. I mean, it can't get any better than giving a lap dance to Whitley. Though the more I look at Trent, I have a feeling that not only is this name not going to die, but that my old friend is up to something no good. And I have another feeling it's at my expense.

"Trent…" I say, my voice growing more impatient. "What the fuck did you do?"

Trent turns his phone to me, and I take a few steps closer to him. I can tell a video is playing, and at first, I'm not sure what it is.

Then I see her hair. That blond hair that I'd know anywhere.

Then I see me, sliding on the floor to her, spreading open her legs. Only when this video was taken, I didn't know what it would feel like to be between those legs.

"Trent. What the fuck is this?" I bark, grabbing the phone from his hand.

"Easy, man. It's nothing to be mad about," Trent says, though his voice doesn't sound as confident as it did a few minutes ago. "I just happened to take a video of you giving the beautiful Miss Whitley a lap dance. And I maybe, as a drunken joke, uploaded it to the ForU app under an account I created called Officer_Sexy. And maybe, just maybe, it has gone viral and my phone has been blowing up all week because of it. Congratulations, my friend, you have officially become a thirst trap."

ForU?

Viral video?

Thirst trap?

I plop down on the high-top stool and just stare at the video, watching it over and over again as I try to process all of this.

I'm not a big social media guy. I have Facebook and Instagram, but I rarely use them. I definitely don't have an app that I only know about because of my niece doing ridiculous dances she learned on there.

I'm definitely not a guy who would ever make a viral video.

And what the fuck is a *thirst trap*?

"Dude, are you mad?" Trent asks, and if I had to guess, he's starting to maybe feel bad about what he did. "You love that kind of attention. I didn't think it would be a big deal."

Am I mad? I don't even know. It's true I don't mind attention. I've never been one to hide in the corner. I'm madder that he did it without my consent.

Then there is Whitley. Is she mad that this video is alive for the *ForU* world to see? Does she even know? Does she think I did it? Does she hate me now?

And, of course, I have no way of knowing how to contact her.

"I… I don't know, man," I say, trying to find the words. "I don't care that you videoed it. I knew people were. But you posted this for the world to see. And apparently it has. And did you think about her at all? That's not cool, man."

"Dude, don't worry," Trent says, taking the phone back from me and ignoring everything I just said. "All of the comments and messages are about you. No one has even mentioned her. And no way can you please all these women in the comments, so I'll take a few off of your hands."

"What do you mean comments and messages?"

Trent laughs, scrolling past the video and going to a page flooded with comments.

And a lot of water emojis, whatever that means.

"He can dance like that for me any day!"

"I'm going to need his location so I can not-so-patiently wait for a dance."

"Does he do private shows?"

"I'm pregnant from watching him. And I've had a hysterectomy."

"Must. Find. Officer. Sexy."

"Can he dance like that horizontally?"

My jaw drops with every comment. And those are the tame

ones. Some of them make my cheeks heat, and it's not easy to embarrass me.

"You should read the direct messages," Trent says. "Those are... let's just say I wish I could move like you, my friend."

I tell him to pull up the messages, and I quickly glance over the words I can see without opening them. Holy hell, he's right.

I want you to...

You are so fucking hot...

I'd like to fuck...

SUBJECT: Whitley

Whitley? I don't even stop to look at who sent it or glance at the user's picture as I open the message. If it has her name in it, I need to read it.

Officer Sexy, huh? I like it. Has a certain ring to it.

Whitley told me you two were going to leave everything in Nashville and remember it as a fun night. Well, Officer Sexy, my girl is miserable, and I have a feeling the only one who can put a smile on her face is you. Here's her number. You didn't get it from me.

By the way, she hasn't seen the video. She doesn't have the app. Just figured you should know that.

— Betsy

8

WHITLEY

THERE ARE pros and cons to being in business for yourself. One of the pros, especially this past week, has been that I don't work with anyone, therefore no one is around to judge me for not wearing makeup or real pants, since I got back from Nashville.

Then there are the cons. Take tonight. Even though I want to just sit at home in my comfy sweatpants and eat an entire cheesecake while binge-watching *New Girl* for the twentieth time, I can't. Tonight is the annual Birmingham City Hospital Fundraiser—also known as the center of my life for the past six months. This is my biggest event of the year. I've been working every connection I've ever made to make this the highest-earning fundraiser in the hospital's history.

Too bad I have no desire to be here.

I especially don't want to be chatting up the who's who of Alabama society—or their douchey sons.

"...And of course, we'd have to see if your dad and brother can come along."

I wasn't paying attention to anything this son of a someone said, but then I heard the words "dad" and "brother" and it snapped me out of my boredom.

Consider those two words my trigger warnings. If a man brings them up in conversation with me, he doesn't want me.

He wants tickets.

Preferably to the Iron Bowl.

"I'm sorry, I missed that last part," I say, curious as to what my dad and brother should come along to. Not because it will happen. Call it curiosity killing the cat.

"Your family and mine taking a weekend getaway down on the Gulf Shores," he says. "It would be great."

I give my head a little shake. "I'm sorry, but have we met before tonight?"

He's taken aback by my question, and just for a second, I worry that I do know him.

Then he opens his mouth again.

"Not technically," he says, his voice not as confident as it was just a minute ago. "Our daddies were in the same class at Alabama. And he's on the board here at the hospital so I just thought maybe we could have dinner, and maybe our families could meet…"

I don't even hear whatever else he said.

He just thought.

Of course, he did. Because, for some reason, this is how men in my circle think things operate. We go out for a date or two before the families meet. Which is all they want, to get to meet my dad.

It's never about me.

Except last week it was.

I don't even excuse myself from the conversation and make my way to the bar as thoughts of Jake float through my head. I've done pretty well tonight. I've only thought about him five times.

That's much better than the rest of the week when it's five times before I've even had breakfast.

It was the right idea to not give him my number. Right? It

would have just dragged out the obvious. Yes, we could have seen each other on the occasional weekends. Maybe meet for a weekend in Nashville. But how long would that have lasted? His life is in Tennessee, and mine is here.

No. This was for the best. It was one amazing night that I'll cherish forever.

Except the problem is, I can still feel his hands on me. I can still feel his lips on my neck. I can still remember the way my body reacted when he made me see stars.

I knew it then, and I know it now: The man has ruined me.

If any other single woman was in my position right now, they'd be trolling this ballroom for men. This room is stacked with the most influential and wealthy people of Alabama, and some of the most eligible bachelors in the entire state. They wear their custom tuxedos like a second skin. They have old southern money that goes back longer than any of us have been alive.

But none of that is doing it for me. All I can think about is the man in plaid and Wranglers who made me feel like I was the only woman in the world.

"What's the matter, Whitley? No one here going to give you a lap dance tonight?"

The sound of Emmilene's voice grates on me like nails on a chalkboard. I was so focused on making sure the final donations for the night were coming through that I let myself forget she was likely going to be here. Her father is the CEO of the biggest bank group in Alabama. And there are single men here. That's like catnip for her.

I take in a deep breath and plaster on the biggest fake smile I can before turning to her. "Hi, Emmilene. Are you having a good time?"

"Why, of course I am. This is much more my scene compared to last weekend."

It takes all I have not to roll my eyes. This is the woman who, just seven days ago, was ready to fuck the entire Nashville Fury if I could have set it up. And I know for a fact she was jealous as all get out that Ella Mae grabbed me instead of her when Jake offered her the dance.

Then there is the fact that she hooked up with Trent that night. Or so Betsy said.

If there is a definition of fake-ass bitch in the dictionary, Emmilene's picture is next to it. And I should know, I was a sorority girl at an SEC school and competed in beauty pageants.

"Your sister had fun, and that's all that matters."

"I mean, she said she did, but I'm not sure. She has to feel so embarrassed," Emmilene says, and even though I don't want her to elaborate, she and I both know I'm going to take the bait.

"And why would you say that?"

Her face lights up at my question. "I know I would be mortified if one of my bridesmaids was shown on a video getting a lap dance from a country bumpkin."

I blink a few times, replaying the words she just said. "What are you talking about?"

Her smile turns sinister. "Why, haven't you seen it? It's quite… scandalous. If I do say so myself. I wonder what your daddy would think of it? And your clients."

Now she's just pissing me off. "What are you talking about, Emmilene?"

"Why, the video, of course. Of you and… oh whatever his name was," she says. "It's all over *ForU*."

ForU? The video app where people are famous for ridiculous reasons? Betsy has it and is addicted to it. She claims to have it for the cooking hacks, but I know the real reason she's on it— the men. She showed me a few videos of men going from geek to hot freak. That's Betsy's kind of crazy.

For me? I've resisted it. I have enough going on. I don't need another social media app sucking time from my day.

"I must say, when I watched it, I almost didn't believe it,"

Emmilene drones on. "I mean, I was there, but I didn't realize until I rewatched it how into it you were. I must say, it wasn't very becoming of you. I wonder what..."

I don't even know what else she says because I sprint out of the ballroom before she can finish.

I make my way to the ladies' room and unceremoniously plop on the couch, taking deep breaths to try and steady myself as a million questions go through my head.

What does it look like?

How long has it been up?

How bad is it? Will I lose clients because of this? Will my family get dragged into the mud for it?

Can you even tell it's me? Or did Emmilene only know because she was there?

And wait, how did she see it? Did it... oh God, is it viral?

I need to see it. Now.

I grab my phone out of my clutch purse and don't even bother sending a text.

"Hello?"

"Send it to me."

Betsy lets out a sigh. "How did you find out?"

"Emmilene."

"That bitch."

"That isn't new information. Enough about her. I need to see it."

"No, you don't."

My eyes grow wide. "What do you mean, I don't need to see it? What if—"

I hear Betsy take a deep breath, like she's gearing up to fight me if need be. "It's been on there for a week. Don't you think if it was bad that I would have sent it to you by now?"

"A week!" I don't even know how loud I scream, but I don't care at this point. "Betsy! That makes it even worse. Send it to me now. Or I swear I'll download the app and watch it for myself. How do you search for it?"

I hear her chuckle. "You try and figure that out for yourself. That's the only way you are going to see it."

I can't believe the words that are coming out of her mouth. She's my best friend. My person. She's the one I'd call if I ever need to bury a body. How is she keeping this from me? Doesn't she realize what this could do if it's as bad as I think it could be?

"Listen, Whitley. I love you. You're my sister from another mister. But you, my darling, never let loose. You always let who you are, or your job, prevent you from living your best life. And last week? I saw the Whit I know you want to be. The one who had fun without thinking about what it would mean for her father or her career. Last week I saw a normal twenty-six-year-old woman having the time of her life with her girlfriends. The one who met a guy and let the night take it wherever it wanted to. The video isn't bad. You had his hat on for most of it. Unless you were there, no one can tell it's you. Emmilene only knows it's you because she was there and she's a cunt bag. Do you truly think that if I thought this was going to damage your life I'd keep it from you?"

I let her words sink in. She wouldn't. I know it in my heart of hearts.

"I still want to see it."

She lets out a small laugh. "Then that's on you. But trust me. You're fine. Plus, I think that video is going to do more good than harm."

"And how do you think that's going to happen?"

"Just a feeling. Bye, babe."

I think I'm more confused now than I was before. But I do know this—I need to see it. I won't be able to do anything else until I do.

But just as I'm about to download the app, I almost drop my phone as the vibration of a text comes through.

A text from a number I don't know.

Without thinking, I open it up. Then I see the first two words, and my body heats up and relaxes all at the same time.

Unknown: Hey, sweetness. Can we talk?

And just like that, watching the video is not on the top of my to-do list.

9

JAKE

WHITLEY: At a thing. Will call you later.

I don't know how many times I've read that text over.

Does she mean it? Is this her polite way of telling me to fuck off? How long is later? What is a thing? Is she on a date?

I head into my kitchen to grab a beer—anything to kill time as I wait for Whitley to, or maybe not, call me back.

Maybe my text was too much? Should I have kept it more casual? Should I have called her sweetness? Just saying, "can we talk?" felt so impersonal. Especially when I'm trying to gauge if she hates me.

I take a hefty pull of my beer. I'm not this guy. I'm not the guy who agonizes over what to say to a woman on a text message. Or the guy who doesn't leave his phone as to not miss a call.

Yes, my attempt in seventh grade of impressing Missy Fisher didn't work, but I'd have to say that since then, my luck with women has improved. Slightly. I'm not Knox, the guy who can walk into a room and have any woman he wants. I'm also not Trent, the man who needs a whole bottle of liquid courage and a wingman to approach someone he's interested in.

Then there is me. I'm the guy who has no problem approaching women, but somehow, I find my way into the friend zone so quickly I never had a chance. One woman I dated said that I was "so easy to talk to, it was like chatting with one of her girlfriends."

That's not what you want to hear from a woman you're trying to sleep with.

I think that's partly why I take every dare I do—especially ones involving women. I don't want to be seen as the friend. I want to be seen as the guy who takes risks—the guy who is a little dangerous. The guy they want to know more about.

The guy who will give you a lap dance when he doesn't even know your name.

The vibration of my phone almost makes me jump out of my seat. I look and see her name on my screen, yet I can't make myself answer. If she hates me, this is going to be the last time I ever talk to her again.

But if she doesn't...

I take one last deep breath and hit the green button. "Hello?"

"Hey, cowboy."

That's not the greeting of someone who hates me. At least, I don't think.

"I told you I'm not a cowboy."

"Semantics."

I can't help but smile, the sound of her voice an immediate balm to my nerves.

"Thanks for calling."

"Should I ask how you got my phone number? Or did you use your super policeman skills to look me up?"

I smile at the teasing in her voice. "A good police officer never reveals his process."

"Betsy gave it to you, didn't she?"

I laugh. "A good police officer also never reveals his informants."

"So, she'll give you my number, but she won't show me the video. Some best friend she is."

Did she just say what I think she said? I figured that she had seen it after Betsy sent that message.

"You haven't seen the video? That was actually why I was calling."

"Oh, I thought maybe…"

"Maybe what?"

"I-I thought maybe you were calling me because of… never mind. It's silly. So about the video."

"We'll get back to the video. Why did you think I was calling you?"

I hate that she thinks right now this is the only reason I'm calling her. Though, without the video, I don't know if we'd be talking right now. But I don't want to assume with her this time. That's what I did last week, and it led to the most miserable seven days of my life.

"I was." I hear her take a breath. "Okay, fine. I was hoping you called me because you wanted to see me again. But if you only called me about the video, then that's fine too and crap on a cracker, now I'm rambling."

I can't help but laugh. "I wish I could see your face right now. I bet you're cute when you ramble."

"Don't change the subject cowboy."

"Okay, okay," I say, relaxing into my couch. "Is one of the reasons why I called you because of the video? Yes. But that's because I just found out about it tonight. Trent posted it. I didn't care about me, but I wanted to make sure you were okay with it being online. Then I found out you didn't know. Which is also how I got your number and… I'm trying to remember right now why we decided to leave everything in Nashville. Because I'm racking my brain and I don't remember one good reason as to why we shouldn't give this a try."

The line falls silent, and I'm almost worried that she isn't there. Then I hear her breathing.

"I think we thought it was for the best," she finally says.

"Can I now go on the record of saying that in retrospect, it was not for the best."

She laughs softly. "In retrospect, I would have to agree. The question is now, cowboy, what do we do with this knowledge?"

I don't answer right away because I want to make sure I get this right. She's in Birmingham. I'm here. It's only a two-hour drive. But I don't care if she was five hours away or in another country. I want this woman in my life. I want to see where this goes. I don't want to go another week wondering what could have been. I want that feeling back, like I had that morning in the hotel room.

"We do have each other's phone numbers now," I begin.

"Yes, we do."

I'm sure if I were to look in a mirror now, I'd look like an idiot for how hard I'm smiling. I couldn't care less. "Then I propose that we take this week to get to know each other. And then, if it's okay with you, the next weekend I have off, I'll drive to Birmingham and spend the weekend with you?"

"You don't have to do that!"

That wasn't the response I hoped for. Then again, I didn't expect her to sound panicked at the thought of seeing me again.

"I don't have to what? Don't you want to see me?"

"I do. I really do. But don't come here," she says, her words rushed. "I mean, you can. Or I can come up there. I'd love to see where you live."

"Are you sure?"

"Absolutely. I think I can get there in a few weeks," she says, her words finally slowing down. "So, we'll talk tomorrow?"

I lie back on my couch, feeling relaxed for the first time in seven days. "Who says we're getting off the phone now?"

I hear what seems to be the sound of bedsprings on the other line. "Good. Because I still want to hear about this video."

10

WHITLEY

WHITLEY: We are out to dinner. What appetizer are you campaigning for?

Jake: That depends. What type of restaurant are we at?

Whitley: Your choice.

Jake: I feel like you are taking the easy way out with that answer.

Whitley: Are you going to answer me or not? The future of our relationship is counting on this question right now.

Jake: Jeez, woman. I didn't know you were this passionate about appetizers.

Whitley: Appetizers are the most important part of the meal. This is a necessary question. Compatibility is necessary. Oh, and don't say the sampler. It's the easy way out.

Jake: I've never talked so much about appetizers in my life.

Whitley: And yet you still haven't answered.

Jake: Fine, since you won't tell me where we are, I'll assume we're either in Birmingham or Rolling Hills. Knowing the dining options in one, and guessing in the other, I'm going to go with fried okra.

Whitley: =) See, was that so hard?

Jake: You are exhausting.

Whitley: Just wait until we transition into ice cream flavors.

————

JAKE: I don't know if we can continue this. It's been nice knowing you.
Whitley: Oh my goodness! All I said was that I'm not a fan of country music!
Jake: How do you call yourself a proper southern woman and not like country music?
Whitley: Because my parents listened to it and it sounded depressing. It was all about trucks and dogs and sad love songs.
Jake: It's so much more than that.
Whitley: Oh really?
Jake: Yes. Now the women are talking about taking bats through the windshields of the men who did them wrong.
Whitley: Why didn't you tell me? That I can get into. Do I get to wear the boots? I think I'd look cute in the boots.
Jake: ....
Whitley: Are you picturing me in just cowboy boots?
Jake: No...
Whitley: Jake...
Jake: Fine. You're also wearing my ball cap.

————

WHITLEY: Kids?
Jake: A whole bunch.
Whitley: Are you the one pushing them out? Because I'm a max three.
Jake: Three is good.
Whitley: Do you have any brothers or sisters? And how am I just asking you this!

Jake: You were asking me the important things like appetizers.

Whitley: It was important.

Jake: Of course it was, sweetness. And I have one sister. Older. She has a son and daughter. Luke is twelve, and Mariah is eight. They are great. She's okay too, I guess.

Whitley: Are you fun Uncle Jake?

Jake: Of course. Especially when they were younger. Sugar them up and send them home. What about you? Siblings? Crazy overprotective brother I need to be aware of?

Whitley: One older brother, but not overprotective. We only see each other a few times a year, so you're good.

I let out a big sigh of relief as Jake changes the topic of conversation from family to a story of something that happened today on his shift.

At least I didn't have to lie to him.

That was the closest I've come to having to finally reveal my last name. Or, he's a unicorn that does know who I am but doesn't care.

Though the more I get to know him, the more I know he truly is one of a kind.

We've been having text conversations like this all week. And each night, we FaceTime before bed. I'm greeted every morning by a good morning text, and somehow, he knows the exact moment each day when I need to get a "thinking of you" message.

How did this man fall into my lap? Literally. Because every time he says something sweet or talks about volunteering to coach little league baseball, I have to pinch myself that he's for real.

Every time we talk, I feel myself falling a little more for this man.

Which scares the heck out of me.

It hasn't even been a full week since we reconnected. We've

only spent one physical night with each other. What if all of this is still wrapped up in the tornado that was the first night we met? I don't know if it is or not. All I do know is that every time I talk to him, there's a smile on my face. And there hasn't been a smile on my face like this in a long time.

Maybe ever.

Speak of the devil…

"Is it already time for our good night FaceTime?"

"No, but texting wasn't doing it for me tonight."

I take a seat on my bed, resting against the headboard. "You're already tired of me?"

"Not even a little. I just got off of work early and wanted to see your gorgeous face."

Swoon.

That's what I want to do. Physically swoon. I want to melt right down off this headboard into a puddle of mush on my bed.

Who says things like this? The answer: he does.

"Quiet night in Rolling Hills?"

This makes him laugh. "It's always a quiet night in Rolling Hills."

"No blue hairs having birthday parties that hired out your services?"

He lets out a groan. "I should have never told you about that."

"I'm glad you did, Officer Sexy. I need to know my competition for when I come to visit. Those two sound like a handful."

"I think you can take them."

I take a second and reposition myself, matching his position with my hand under my head. When I'm finally situated, I can't help but notice him staring.

"You okay?"

I don't know what he is staring at, but he must have been in a trance because my words visibly startle him.

"Jake, are you okay? If you're tired, we can talk tomorrow."

He gives his head a little shake. "I'm fine. Just a bit distracted."

I quirk an eyebrow. "By what?"

He takes a breath and looks back to me. "I'm going to sound like a douche when I say this, and I'd like to go on the record for saying that I'm not this kind of guy."

"Now I have to know."

"I also preface this with I have been a perfect gentleman these past few nights, but tonight... when you just laid down... your boobs... they are... right there. And I miss them. And if I'm going to be completely honest, I want them in my mouth."

My eyes grow wide when I realize what he's seeing. But there they are, as clear as the water in Gulf Shores, my girls pressed together like they are ready to bust through my sleep tank.

"Oh gosh!" I say, quickly repositioning myself.

"Don't you dare."

His words come out deep and bossy, and it transports me back to that first night together. And now I'm remembering what that glorious mouth did to my breasts and the rest of me that night.

I turn myself back to the position I was just in, loving how his eyes are filled with nothing but lust.

"You want me to stay like this?" I say, giving the girls a little extra push together.

"Actually, I want to see them. Take off your shirt, sweetness."

Between the deep tone of his voice and the way he is looking at me right now, I'm pretty sure I would do anything this man asked me. Though that doesn't calm the nerves about what he's asking me to do.

If this were any other man, I'd never even consider this. But this is Jake. The man who made me feel ways I never thought I could feel. The man who I trusted enough to give myself to after only knowing him a few hours.

The man who I think I could fall in love with one day.

I sit up, bringing the phone with me as I use one hand to bring up the bottom of my shirt. Somehow, I manage to take it off without dropping the phone.

"Is this what you wanted?"

If I thought there was lust in Jake's eyes before, right now, there is outright fire.

"Damn right, it is," he says, turning so now he's lying flat on his back. "God, I miss you."

I don't know what makes me do what I do next. Maybe it's his words or the look that he's giving me. Either way, it's making me feel bold in a way I've never felt before.

I cup one of my breasts with my free hand, letting my fingers play with my nipple. I've never been big on pleasuring myself, and right now, I'm wondering why. I feel amazing. Powerful. Beautiful.

Or maybe it's the way Jake is looking at me. His eyes are heavy, hungry, like he could eat me up. Or possibly lick me half to death again. The thought of his mouth on me again sends a little curl of pleasure through my stomach. I squeeze my thighs together, trying to ignore how wet he makes me, even from a hundred-some miles away.

A muscle tics in his jaw as he watches me. "You're squirming, sweetness. You all right?"

"Yes." I try to sound convincing, but my voice sounds wobbly. "You're still wearing your shirt, that's not fair."

Jake smirks at me, propping himself up on one elbow and leaning into the camera. "Then tell me what you want, Whitley."

Oh, jeez. I have to say it?

"Take off your shirt." I breathe.

"Yes, ma'am." Jake's drawl thickens as he watches me roll my nipple between my fingers. He mutters a soft curse under his breath as he sits up. He reaches one arm back behind his head, the muscles bunching in his bicep as he grabs the back of his T-shirt and pulls it off over his head in one fluid motion.

"Oh, sweet Jesus." I moan quietly. He's every inch as sexy as I remember. His abs flex as he reclines back on his elbow, and as he does, I can see the thick outline of his erection straining against the front of his sweatpants.

"Are you… Oh," I say awkwardly. Duh. He's definitely turned on. But that's kind of a given since I have my boobs out.

Jake lifts an eyebrow, smiling wryly at my wide-eyed expression. He presses a palm against the front of his sweatpants.

"You've gotta stop looking at me like that, Whitley. You're making my situation… difficult."

"Were you going to say 'hard'?" I ask with a laugh. Jake shrugs, grinning at me shamelessly.

I bite my lip, trying to be bold. "Maybe I want to make your situation *hard*."

"Take off the shorts." Jake's deep command rumbles over me, sending a little shiver up my spine.

"I'm not wearing any underwear," I admit, my eyes following the movement of his hand. He's given up trying to suppress his hard-on, and now his fingers are tracing the length slowly, deliberately, and the sight seems to steal the air from my room.

"Good," he growls. "Take them off. I want to see what I've been missing."

"Okay." I laugh nervously. "Hang on." I prop my phone against a pillow, adjusting the angle. Jake watches me, his lips parted and eyelids heavy with lust as I slip my thumbs under the elastic of my sleep shorts, sliding them down my hips slowly. My heart races as I get them down my thighs. I've never done this, and I'm shaking with adrenaline. I can't even tell if it's nerves or excitement at this point.

"Good girl," he says, his hand continuing to stroke his length. "Spread your legs. Show me how wet you are."

I do as he says, allowing my finger to find my center. "So wet. Now show me your cock."

Did I just say that? Who is this woman? Certainly not prim and proper Whitley McAvoy, who didn't let a boy feel her up until college.

I continue to coat my fingers in my wetness as Jake quickly strips off his sweatpants and boxer briefs. His cock springs free, and he quickly takes it back in his hand, stroking it faster than before.

"Fuck, Whitley," he says, his voice deeper than I've ever heard it. "I'm not going to last. You look so fucking hot."

"I want to come Jake; make me come."

My fingers find my clit, and I rub it furiously, aching for release. It's too much right now. The feeling of my hands touching myself, the dirty words we are saying to each other, the sight of him pleasuring himself because of me… it's all too much.

"See this cock, Whitley? Remember how it fucked you? How it made you scream?"

"Yes," I say breathlessly, my hands now rubbing at my center furiously.

"Scream for me, sweetness. Scream for me now."

The sound of his dirty words is enough to send me over the edge. My core clenches, and just like that, I explode on my hand.

"Oh fuck! Whitley!"

I hear Jake's groan as I ride the wave of my orgasm.

Holy hell, that was the hottest thing I've ever done in my life.

Neither of us says anything for a minute, both just lying back on our beds, looking at each other on our phones. Did that just happen? Did I just have FaceTime sex?

I don't know what this man is doing to me. All I know is that I want more of it.

"That was unexpected," I say, still trying to catch my breath.

"That it was, sweetness," he says, his eyes fluttering shut. "I can't wait to do it again."

I laugh, feeling the exhaustion hit me as well. "How about we wait until we can do it for real?"

This earns me a smile. "Ten days."

I'm counting the minutes already.

11

JAKE

"DUDE, YOU'RE LATE."

I don't even bother responding to Trent as I toss my gym bag on the floor.

"Who the hell pissed in your Wheaties?"

"No one," I snap, grabbing weights to put on the bar. "Are we going to lift or not?"

I hate that I'm snapping at Trent, but I can't help it.

I should be in a good mood. No, a *great* mood. Between the FaceTime sex last night and the picture Whitley sent me this morning that made me take an extra shower, I should be walking on air.

"Are you going to tell me why you're salty as fuck today, or am I going to have to guess?" Trent asks. "Things not going well with Whitley? If you need pointers on how to keep a woman satisfied, all you have to do is ask."

I give him a shove as I position myself at the bench press station. "Whitley and I are just fine. And you are the last person I'd come to for relationship advice. But if you must know, I just came from my mom's house."

"Why's that bad? Your mom is great. Pretty hot, too."

I shoot him a death glare. "I'd rather you not talk about my mom. Ever."

All he does is shrug. Asshole. "Then tell me what the bug is up your ass. You're no fun when you're grumpy."

I grunt, pushing through my set. "She said there was a leak in the roof. So I went over to fix it. Turns out the entire roof is about to collapse. She needs a new one. Stat."

"That sucks," Trent says, switching with me to do his set. "How much is that going to cost?"

"That's the problem," I say, taking off a few of the weights for him. "She had to have her septic tank fixed a few months ago. That wiped out her savings."

"Can you or your sister help?"

I let out a defeated sigh, having already played all this out in my head. "Yes, but I don't want to ask Amelia. She doesn't get any child support from her dead-beat ex-husband. I don't want to take a penny of her money that she needs for the kids. This one is going to fall on me."

"But didn't you just cash in your savings to buy your new truck?"

"Ding-ding-ding, you're the winner," I snark. "Now, if you want to win the grand prize, figure out a way that I can make a quick five grand."

At the time, I thought I was being responsible. I worked every overtime shift I could get and saved every extra penny to buy my truck outright. The thought of working overtime right now sounds miserable. I'd rather spend that time talking to Whitley or maybe taking some time off I've earned to drive to Birmingham to spend time with her.

Can I go back to last night when she was fingering herself for me? I'd much rather be back there.

"Okay, I'm going to say something crazy, and I want you to hear me out."

I raise an eyebrow at Trent because I have a feeling I'm not going to like what is about to come out of his mouth. "The fact that I'm going to listen to you right now after you start the conversation like that shows how desperate I am."

He finishes his set and sits up. "Did you know that you now have one million followers on *ForU*?"

"Say that again?"

"Officer Sexy. He has one million followers on *ForU*. Turns out your moves are pretty popular."

One million? Damn. I might not be on social media, but even I know one million is a lot.

"That's great. But what does that have to do with me making money to get Mom a new roof?"

He reaches down into his gym bag and pulls out his phone. "I might have checked the messages the other day, and dude, companies are begging to work with you. I think you could make some money off of this."

I shake my head, trying to process his words right now. "Dude. Nothing you are saying makes sense."

He shoves his phone into my hand. "Just look. I think you could make some serious money."

I take the phone out of his hand and open the first message, still skeptical about everything he is saying.

We would love for you to do a dance to this song for one of our up-and-coming artists. Payment is $300 for a one-minute video.

I give my head a little shake. Three hundred dollars for dancing to a song? Is this for real?

I open up message after message. Some are from women who are... let's just say I never want Whitley to see these messages.

But between those are what Trent said, messages from companies wanting to work with me.

Holy hell.

"And that's not the only part," Trent says, taking his phone back as I sit stunned that this is even a possibility. "There is this program through the app. You sign up and you get paid per video view. Dude, I think you could make the money in a few months. Easy."

I give him a sideways glance. "How the hell do you know all of this?"

He just shrugs his shoulders. "For as much as my phone has been blowing up the past few days because of notifications from this app, let's just say I'm now invested in your career. I'm like your agent."

"You could have deleted it."

"I could have, but then, how could I be helping you now? Admit it. I'm your hero. Your financial savior."

"I wouldn't go that far," I say, taking the phone back to read the messages again. "It seems too good to be true."

Could this work? I look at some of the messages and what they are asking. It doesn't seem that hard, and if I'm doing my calculations right, I could earn money quick. And a lot less work than an overtime shift.

But will it work? If I'm going to do this, and that's still a big if, I need to know it's going to work. I don't have time to waste. Mom's roof isn't collapsing, yet, but it's one good storm from falling in.

"How about this," Trent says, sensing my hesitation. "Let's make a video right now. I'll film. Let's see how many views it gets. Then you make your decision."

I look around the gym. We aren't alone. A few high school kids are lifting a few spots down from us. A Pilates class is going on, and Daisy and Doris are slowly walking on a treadmill. I'm definitely *not* dancing in front of them.

"Fine, but not here."

Trent smiles. "I have the perfect place."

———

"HOW IS THIS THE PERFECT PLACE?"

"What?" he says, looking around like I'm crazy. "This is perfect."

I look around at the old basketball court that's attached to our gym, unable to hold back a sneeze. "It's dusty. And dirty. And I'm pretty sure no one has been here since we were five."

Trent looks around but doesn't seem to have the same worries I do. "It has ambiance. And it's private. You don't have to worry about anyone walking in."

That's true. I didn't even know you could still get in here. And as much as I want to know how Trent knows, at the same time, I don't. I have a feeling I might have to arrest him if I did.

"Okay, what do I have to do?"

Trent perks up. "I love this. It's like I'm your manager. Agent/Manager Trent Martin."

I roll my eyes. "Whatever you need to call yourself. Just tell me what to do."

He scrolls on his phone a minute before playing a song. I've heard it, though I can't put my finger on where. It's not my cup of tea, but it has a good beat.

"This song is all over the app right now. I've read that if you use popular songs, you have the chance to get more video views. And for you my friend, that means more money."

"You read?"

He ignores my jab. "Focus, Evans. All you need is to dance in your Officer Sexy way for thirty-six seconds. That's the length of this song. Do whatever you want. Leave the rest to me."

"Leave the rest to me" are the five worst words Trent could ever say. Usually, that only means trouble, and that's the last thing I need in my life right now.

"Are you sure this is going to work?" I ask, still a bit hesitant.

"We won't know until you try. Now let's do this, Officer Sexy. Show us those moves that have made you famous."

I take a deep breath and give myself one more internal pep talk.

This is for Mom.

This is innocent entertainment.

Except I kind of feel like a prostitute.

I shake away that last thought as I hear Trent countdown to starting the video.

3...

2...

1...

Here goes nothing.

I hear the first bass drop of the song, and my hips immediately go into action. I don't know how I'm doing it. The only logical way of explaining it is that I'm letting the music take over my body. It's something I've always been able to do, though I've never told anyone that. I guess those dance lessons way back paid off more than I thought.

Before I know it, I feel myself reaching behind my head, pulling my T-shirt off in one swift motion. I toss it to the side before turning my body to jump into a handstand, slowly lowering myself to the floor before sliding to my knees.

Sliding to my knees...

Whitley... the lap dance.

That's where I've heard this song before. At one of the bars in Nashville. Whitley and I were standing at the bar when it came on, and without even knowing it, we started dancing together, our hips finding each other with every beat.

Thoughts of Whitley are now in my mind as I continue moving to the music. I have no idea how long I've been going or how much more of the song is left. All I know is that my body has a mind of its own right now. Thoughts of her blond hair are spurring me on, making my hips move up and down in a way I didn't know they could.

"Done!" Trent yells, breaking me from my trance. "Dude, I'd

like to say right now that I'm one-hundred percent straight, but that made me question a few things."

"Shut up," I say, standing up and looking around for my discarded shirt. "So what happens now?"

He doesn't answer for a bit, instead typing something on his phone before he slips it back into this pocket. "Now we wait."

12

WHITLEY

I HAVE LIVED a blessed twenty-six years on this planet. However, in none of those years could I say that I had a healthy, functioning relationship with a man. Not in any phases of my life did I date anyone who I thought I could spend the rest of my life with. Heck, I've never even brought a man home to meet my parents.

Then I met Jake.

Yes, I know that we are only two weeks into our long-distance relationship. Yes, I know that we still have only seen each other once. And yes, I know we still have a lot to figure out.

But I also know I've never smiled this much. And that's coming from a former beauty queen.

"Seriously, I can't look at you anymore. It's like you're shitting rainbows twenty-four seven."

I toss a bag of candies at Betsy, which misses her as she ducks with ease. "Don't hate. Plus, this is your fault."

"I couldn't stand you moping around anymore. So, this was the poison I picked."

"Well, I appreciate you," I say, picking up another mesh bag to fill with the exact amount of assorted candies as we've been instructed to do per Ella Mae. "All I want to do is finish these up so I can go home and pack."

"I don't know why you need to pack," Betsy says, tying a bow on her own bag of candy. "Not like you two are going to be wearing clothes at all this weekend."

That thought only makes my smile grow wider. In less than twenty-four hours—ten hours and fourteen minutes to be exact —I am getting in my car and driving to a town I had never heard of two weeks ago. Heck, I'd drive to North Dakota if that's where he was.

I miss him.

I miss him a lot.

And not just the sex. I didn't memorize what it felt like to have his arms around me. I want to feel what his kisses are like when we aren't against the running clock of one night. I want to hold his hand and go get dinner like a normal couple.

Damn, I have it bad.

"What are you packing for?"

The sound of Emmilene's exasperating voice immediately dampens the mood. When Ella Mae asked Betsy and me to come over to help her put together some table favors, we were happy to help. What kind of bridesmaids would we be if we said no?

We thought we were getting an Emmilene free night. We were wrong.

"Whitley is going to see her Officer Sexy boyfriend this weekend," Betsy says, wagging her eyebrows for good measure.

Emmilene lets out a disgusted grunt as she takes a seat across from Betsy and me. "I can't believe you're dating him. That's so—"

"Romantic?" Ella Mae says, joining us in the living room. "And just imagine if I hadn't pushed you two together? It's like something straight out of a romance book!"

"Or porn," Emmilene mumbles just loud enough for us to hear it.

That's it. I can't take it anymore. This bitch has gotten on my last nerve.

"Not that it's any of your business, but would you like to tell me why you have such a problem with my relationship with Jake?"

Emmilene pretends to look shocked for a second before she rights herself. "All I'm saying is that you're a southern woman with ties to the community and around the state. You're a name, Whitley. And you... frankly, the fact that you're slumming it with a man who takes his shirt off on the Internet is quite scandalous."

You've got to be kidding me. This is still about the video? "You need to get over that, Emmilene. It was one video. It was a bachelorette party. No one in the city of Birmingham besides the three of us even know it was me."

Emmilene's eyes shoot up. "You mean you don't know?"

What is she talking about? "Know what?"

As soon as the words leave my mouth, I already know I'm not going to like whatever it is she has to tell me. All I need to do is look at the smile she's wearing. It's like the one Cruella DeVil has when she sees a dalmatian.

Emmilene takes out her phone, plays with it a second before passing it to me. "It's not the only video. I'm just so sorry you have to find out this way. I feel like I'm just always delivering bad news to you."

Against my better judgment, I take Emmilene's phone and look at the screen. Right in front of me is Jake—I'd know that smile anywhere—and I don't know how to describe what I'm watching.

He's dancing, though this time there is no one in a chair on the receiving end.

His hips are mesmerizing.

And the fact that he's shirtless, oh, holy hell.

Just watching this video is making me thirsty.

For water or for him, I'm not sure.

And this is why they call it a thirst trap.

The video ends, and I exit out, only to find out this isn't the only one. In fact, there are five other videos on Officer_Sexy's profile.

All dancing.

All shirtless.

All with at least one million views.

"Did you know about this?" I turn to ask Betsy, who has since ripped the phone from my hand.

"I haven't been on the app in a few days," she says, staring a little too hard for my liking at my boyfriend humping the ground. "I swear I would have told you."

I take the phone back and watch every video again.

I can't lie that I'm not turned on by his performance. It's sexy. Provocative. Especially because I know what's under those jeans that ride down to the perfect spot on his hips.

And now hundreds of thousands of women want to see what's in those jeans.

And I don't know how I feel about that.

I never thought I was the jealous type. Then again, I've never had anything or anyone to ever be jealous about. I guess you truly don't know how you'll react in a situation until you're there.

And now that I'm here, I still don't know.

But I bet I will by the time I drive two hours to Rolling Hills.

I toss the phone back to Emmilene and quickly stand up.

"Where you going?" Betsy asks, a little shocked at my sudden movements.

I hurry and grab my phone and take my keys out of my purse. "I'm going to Rolling Hills. I need to go find out why my boyfriend became a thirst trap and neglected to tell me."

13

JAKE

"HEY, OFFICER SEXY, LOOKING GOOD TONIGHT."

I try not to audibly groan when I hear those words. And not because it's someone calling me Officer Sexy.

It's because they are coming from the mouth of Krystal Shaw.

All I wanted to do was grab a bite to eat and a beer after spending the last few hours getting everything ready for Whitley to arrive tomorrow. And now I have to deal with the town bicycle.

I know that's not very gentlemanly of me to say. But I'm never one to not call a spade a spade. I don't know what it's like to *ride the ride* per se. But Knox does. He doesn't regret much, but he regrets that drunken night after the summer festival when we were twenty-two.

"Why are you calling me that, Krystal?" I ask, making sure not to turn on my barstool. That would give her an opening, and I've been around long enough to see her in action. When she wants something, she's a woman determined.

"Isn't that your name now?" she asks, and I can feel her scooting her barstool closer to me. That and I'm immediately flooded with the smell of her perfume that makes me want to gag.

"Krystal, I'm still the same Jake you've known since first grade. Nothing has changed."

"But you're famous now! All these years I've known you and I had *no* idea you could move like that. And here I was chasing after Knox when it turns out you are the one who has moves for days. I'd love to see them sometime."

She takes her finger and slowly starts moving her fake nail up and down my arm. Even if I wasn't with Whitley, I would still have the exact same reaction—utter disgust.

"Krystal, I'm not interested."

Either she didn't hear me or doesn't care—I'm going with the latter—as she stands up so she can wrap her hands around my arm and press her chest to me.

"Why not, Officer Sexy? I want to know if you move like that without your clothes on."

"He does."

The third voice throws me off for a second because I don't know what's happening right now. I swear that's Whitley's voice. So either she is here early and somehow found me here, or I'm going insane.

I turn my barstool around, and there she is, in the beautiful flesh, my Whitley.

And she looks pissed.

"And who are you?" Krystal says, letting go of my arm so she can go toe-to-toe with Whitley.

"I'm Jake's girlfriend," she says, hands now placed on her hips. "Now, I don't want a fight tonight. And he did ask you nicely to let go of his arm. So why don't you be a dear and leave us alone."

Whitley's twang is stronger than ever, and I'm pretty sure she's going for passive-aggressive southern woman mean, which in my opinion is the scariest kind of mean.

I should know; that's my mom in a nutshell.

"Jake, who is this bitch?" Krystal asks, clearly not understanding what's going on here. I don't even have a chance to answer.

"Oh bless your heart," Whitley says, and yup, there's nothing quite like getting cut down by a southern woman.

Whitley doesn't yell back. Instead, she walks up so close to Krystal you'd think she was whispering in her ear. She's so close and is talking so quietly I can barely hear her.

"Sweetheart, you have no idea who you are talking to. And you certainly should not be calling *me* a bitch. I mean, I'm not the one throwing myself at a man who clearly does not want you. Now, I'm going to ask you one more time, real nicely, to get away from Jake and take your trailer trash, fake tit self away from here. And if I catch you hanging on him again, I'm going to make sure everyone here sees first-hand what you look like without those trashy hair extensions. Do I make myself clear?"

Krystal takes a step back, looks at me, then Whitley again, who is now wearing a smile so big you'd have no idea that she just told this girl off.

"Whatever," Krystal says, grabbing her purse off the bar. "She's not even that pretty. Call me when you're done with *her*."

She turns on her heel and storms out of The Joint. As soon as she steps out, a round of applause I've never heard comes roaring from inside.

"What are you doing here?" I ask, leaning in to give her a kiss as sounds of cheers begin to fade. But instead of tasting her lips, all I'm met with is her index finger, blocking my access.

I don't know what I was expecting the first time I saw her again. But even if I had a hundred scenarios thought up, I definitely wouldn't have picked this.

"We have to talk, *Officer Sexy*."

My eyes grow wide at the use of the name.

The name I never told her.

Fuck my life.

It's not that I wasn't going to tell her about my decision to start making videos. It's that I didn't think it was a conversation to have over the phone. And since she was coming here this weekend, and she didn't have the app, I figured that I had time to do it when she was here.

I was wrong.

"I can explain—"

She opens up her mouth to respond, and if she does, I don't hear her. All I know is that someone is grabbing my shoulder and shoving me out of the way.

"See! I told y'all! It's Whitley McAvoy! Y'all! Whitley McAvoy is here! In person! And she just told that girl off!"

It takes me a second to realize one of the men who shoved me is now standing between my girl and me. And it's not just him. There are three. And they are looking at Whitley like they are seeing a celebrity in real life.

"Whitley, can we get a picture?" one guy says. "Is your brother here? How awesome would that be if Hunter McAvoy were here?"

"Do you know any inside info about the Fury? Is Bryce coming back next season? Where did he go?"

"Screw the Fury. How's your dad? I bet he can still sling that football. Damn. This is the best night ever! Guys! This woman is football royalty! And she can win a cat fight!"

Their questions don't settle down, and even though I'm standing right next to them, it's like I'm on the outside looking in to an alternate reality.

The Nashville Fury? Football royalty? What are they talking about?

Whitley isn't football royalty. I mean, I don't think she is. Now that I come to think of it, I don't know who Whitley is. Yes, we've talked about a lot of things, but every time we get close to talking about her family life, she shuts down. I just figured she had a rough childhood and didn't want to talk about it yet.

Whitley McAvoy.

I roll the name around in my head before it hits me. Holy hell, is she related to the football coach of the Nashville Fury? He was a big deal at Alabama. I'm not even a Crimson Tide fan, but I know that. Hell, he made my team's life miserable for four years. And if memory serves me right, his dad was a damn good player too.

These guys are right. She is football royalty.

I just stare at her as she politely takes a few selfies with these strangers. I might have been keeping a secret about myself, but it turns out I'm not the only one.

————

SILENCE.

That's all it has been since we left The Joint.

Not a word as we walked to my truck.

Not in the ten-minute drive back to my house.

Not since she's come in and sat on my couch.

And it's killing me.

"So which one of us is going to go first?" I say, cutting the silence as I sit next to her. I make sure to keep my distance. I hate it, but I have no idea what's going on in her head right now.

She doesn't look at me, instead fixating on the hemline of her shirt. "I had this whole speech ready to go about you hiding something from me. And how this wasn't going to work if we weren't honest with each other. I guess I forgot that I was hiding something as well."

"Why didn't you tell me who you were?"

She takes a long, deep breath before beginning. "Do you know you're my first real relationship?"

I wasn't expecting that. "I am? I mean, I'm not calling you a liar, but I can't believe that you… how can that be?"

She takes a breath, still focusing on the damn hemline of her shirt. I want her to look at me, but I don't want to push her, either.

"When I was thirteen, I thought I was head over heels for this boy. He was cute, and he got me a carnation from the school fundraiser for Valentine's Day. He even walked me to and from each of my classes. I thought he liked me just as much as I liked him. It was your classic middle school crush."

She takes a breath, but I don't dare say anything. I just give her hand a squeeze.

"Then came the spring dance, and I for sure thought he was going to ask me. My friends even heard him talking about it. They heard wrong. Because instead of asking me to the dance, he asked me if I could get him and his dad Alabama spring game tickets."

"What a little fucking piece of shit," I say. Who the hell did this kid think he was?

"That was the first time something like that happened, but it wasn't the last. Every guy I started talking to, it was only a matter of time before my dad, or my brother, or Alabama football came up. None of them wanted me for me. Or if they did, it was for bragging rights that they were dating a beauty queen. So I quit trying. Dating wasn't worth it if I had to constantly wonder if they were in it for me or they just wanted to date me because of my family. Then you came along."

She takes another breath, but this time she's the one who moves closer, taking my free hand in hers. "When I went to Nashville, I was just Whitley. You didn't recognize me. You liked me for me. I didn't have to wonder. It felt good. I guess I just didn't want that feeling to end, or if you would look at me diff—"

I cut off her words with a kiss. One, because she's been with me for hours now and I haven't felt her lips against mine and that's unacceptable. And two, because I need to kiss that thought right out of her beautiful head.

"You listen to me," I say, breaking away just enough so I can say what I need to. "I don't care if you are the Princess of England. I don't care if you are the president's daughter or that your brother is a big-wig football coach. All I care about is you. Because you, sweetness, are the only one for me."

This gets me the smile I've been aching to see all night. "So that girl earlier?"

I let out a deep laugh. "Krystal? Not even a little bit. Let's just say she'd done her tour around town, and I am proud to say that she's never made a stop here."

My explanation doesn't get the reaction I'm hoping for. Instead, she goes back to playing with the hemline of her shirt.

"What's the matter? Talk to me, Whit."

"I…" she pauses, and I can see the wheels turning in her head. "The videos. I need to know, Jake. Why are you making them? And why didn't you tell me?"

It's now my turn to confess. "I had no intention of doing it. I swear I didn't. But my mom needs a new roof, and she's a little low on cash right now. Trent told me how much money I could make on the app. Whit, she's going to have a new roof by the end of this month. And, well, it's kind of fun."

"Fun?" she asks, clearly not prepared for me to say that. "How is taking off your shirt and dancing on the Internet fun?"

"It's not about that," I say, bringing her close to me, hoping that what I'm saying will make sense to her. "You know I love to dance. That night in Nashville, that was me being my true self. I'm the guy who likes to dance and be out there for people to watch. And if it makes me a little money to help out my mom and makes some people smile along the way, then I call that a win-win."

"I believe the app calls it being a thirst trap."

"Is that what they are calling me?" I say, a hint of teasing to my voice. "The beauty queen and the thirst trap. A match made in heaven."

This gets me the laugh I've wanted. I take the opportunity and bring her to my lap.

"Are you okay with me making the videos?" I ask. I would hate to stop, but I can find other ways to make money if it bothers her that much.

"If you enjoy it, I don't want to tell you how to live your life. I just…" she pauses for a second, gathering her words. "I didn't realize how jealous I was going to be of the women who were commenting on the videos. They are aggressive. Then I saw Krystal tonight and I lost it a bit."

"Come here," I say, bringing our mouths together again. This kiss isn't deep, but I hope she can feel what I'm trying to say through it. "You're the only one for me. Those women commenting? They are strangers. They will never know the real me. You? You are real. You know me. The real me. And you're the only one who gets to see my moves in real life, you get me?"

She smiles, her finger beginning to trace up and down my rib cage. "Does being the girlfriend of a thirst trap get me private showings?"

I pick her up slightly, so she's now straddling me. She loops her arms around my neck, and for the first time since she arrived in Rolling Hills, I find myself breathing easier. "That depends. Does being the boyfriend of football royalty get me tickets to the Iron Bowl?"

This takes her back. "I thought you said you weren't an Alabama fan?"

I bring up her shirt, kissing my way across her chest, hoping this will ease the blow I'm about to deliver.

"I'm not. I'm an Auburn fan."

14

WHITLEY

I DON'T KNOW how this day can be any more perfect. I'm on cloud nine, and I'm not even the one getting married.

There isn't a cloud in the sky, and by some miracle, it's not ninety-nine degrees despite it being the middle of July in Alabama. Ella Mae let each of the bridesmaids pick their own style of dress to make up for the fact that Emmilene selected the most hideous color on the chart. I went with a strapless A-line, and it's almost making me forget that it's in puke green.

And then there is my date. If I thought Jake was hot in a plaid shirt and Wranglers, then I don't have a word to describe what he looks like now in his navy suit and white shirt. I can't help but stare at him as he gets us a drink from the bar. He's freshly shaven, his brown hair is styled perfectly, and I might have drooled a little when I saw him at the church today.

I also might have been remembering how he made me scream just a few hours before when we were getting ready at my apartment. Who knew my bathroom counters were so durable?

I let my gaze shift from Jake to everyone on the dance floor. The happiness is contagious as I take in the scene before me.

Ella Mae and her husband are blissfully swaying to the beat of their own drum. The song playing right now is an upbeat pop song, but they are in their own moment, and no one is daring to interrupt them.

Betsy currently has her ass shaking in front of one of the single groomsmen, which I totally called last night when I saw them at the bar together. Heck, even Emmilene seems to be having a good time. That has to be some sort of miracle.

Then there is me. I don't know if happy is a strong enough word to describe what I'm feeling right now. This past month with Jake has been like nothing I've ever known. Yes, we've spent more of it apart than together, but the times when we have been together, we've made sure to soak up every second. And that isn't code for naked and fucking each other's brains out.

We've gotten to know each other, and not just the superficial things like appetizer choices. I know that he might give Knox and Trent a hard time, but those three are as ride-or-die as they come. In turn, he knows that I might dread being only accepted and liked because of my last name but that I wouldn't trade my family for all the money in the world.

I also now truly know how much he loves making videos and putting smiles on people's faces, even if it is doing it half-naked. I have also come to the realization that his followers only know Officer Sexy.

I know Jake. And I know the difference.

"A pretty woman such as yourself should not be sitting here alone. Especially when there is a dance floor just a few feet away."

I let the sound of Jake's voice wash over me before I turn to face him. Just like that first night we met, his voice still gives me shivers every time. Part of me hopes that feeling never goes away.

God, I have it bad for this man.

"Are you asking me to dance?" I say, turning to look at him over my shoulder.

He leans in, his breath on my neck sending chills all through me. "I figured this time I'd give you the choice."

"Is there a chair involved?" I ask, tilting my neck to the side, hoping he gets the hint.

"That dance is tonight, sweetness. Right now, I just want to hold the most beautiful girl here in my arms."

He places a kiss on my neck and pulls my chair out, taking my hand as I stand up, and we make our way to the dance floor. I can feel eyes on us as he pulls me close to his body, his arms snaking around my waist as I loop mine around his neck. The song playing is one about loving all of someone, faults and all, and how that person can't imagine their life without them.

"Do you believe in love like this?" I ask, though I don't know if he hears me considering my head is resting on his chest.

"I believe that if you truly love someone, nothing else matters," he says before bringing my chin up to look at him. "A feeling like love? That doesn't happen every day. Some people spend their entire lives searching for that feeling. For that person that makes them feel complete. So I believe that once they find it, you make it work. Because that feeling—this feeling —you don't let it go, no matter the obstacles."

My eyes go wide at what I think he just said.

Did he just?

Did he just say?

"Jake…"

He smiles before leaning down and pressing a soft kiss to my lips. When he releases them, I don't even need him to say anything. I see everything in his eyes.

This man loves me.

And I am head over heels in love with this man.

I know it's quick. I know it's insane. I know we have a million and a half things to figure out. But I know that what I feel for this man isn't normal. I know it's like nothing I've ever felt.

I'm in love with Jake Evans.

———

"I BELIEVE I PROMISED SOMEONE A DANCE."

I smile as I see Jake standing against the doorframe to my bedroom, the top few buttons of his dress shirt undone and his jacket discarded somewhere. If I had my way, we would have left as soon as Jake and I said the words that we didn't actually say. I didn't realize I was dating a responsible man who reminded me that it wouldn't be good to leave one of my best friend's weddings before the cake was even cut.

So we stayed. We danced. We drank. We had an amazing night.

And the second it was okay to leave, we hightailed it out of there so fast I'm pretty sure we left literal clouds of dust.

"I do believe I remember you saying that," I say as I sit on my bed, carefully taking off the high heels.

"Don't," he says, his voice stopping my movements. "Leave those on."

I look at Jake, who is beginning to unbutton his shirt. "You want me to leave on my heels?"

"The heels that have been driving me fucking crazy all night? Yes. And the jewelry. Take off your dress. Leave the rest to me."

Oh, my word, dirty talking Jake might be my favorite Jake.

"I might need some help with that," I say, slowly standing up and turning my back to him.

I feel him before he even touches me. His fingers gently move my hair to the side, giving him access to my skin that is begging for his touch. He puts gentle kisses across my shoulders before taking my zipper in his fingers, lowering it ever so slowly.

As soon as he gets it down, my dress pools at my feet, showing him what he wanted to see—me standing there in only my heels and jewelry.

"Fuck, Whitley. Have you been walking around all day in this dress without anything on underneath?"

I look over my shoulder, needing to see Jake's reaction right now. "I couldn't have panty lines, now, could I?"

The sound he makes can only be best described as a grunt as he scoops me up under my legs, sitting me back on the bed. I can't help but let out a small laugh as I bounce from the force.

"You think it's funny?" he says, taking a few steps away from me. "You think it's funny teasing me like this?"

"You mean how you tease me and all those women with your videos?" I ask, letting my legs part a little wider. "You're the definition of a tease, cowboy."

He lets his eyes linger on my center, which is getting wetter by the second, before we make eye contact again. His gaze is burning into me as he quickly undoes his belt, pulling it off in one swift movement. He begins stalking toward me, his eyes never leaving mine as he makes his way to the end of the bed.

He stops at the edge, the belt now formed into two loops. "You think this is a tease?" he asks, making sure I'm looking at him as he takes each of my wrists and puts them in the loops. He doesn't break eye contact as he takes the end of the belt and pulls it together with his teeth.

"I..." I can't find my words. I don't know if I'm supposed to speak or let him run the show. Though I have a feeling, no matter what, I'm going to be left speechless.

"You wanted a show, sweetness? Then a show you'll get."

Jake takes a step back, slowly unbuttoning the rest of his shirt. His hips are beginning to move like there's a song playing, though the only sound I hear now is my heavy breathing.

He tosses the shirt before unbuttoning his pants, pushing them to the floor in one swift motion. I want to reach out and touch him, but he's too far away. Plus, I'd have to touch him with both hands as they are currently bound together.

He takes a few steps closer to me, his hard length begging for release from his boxer briefs. I lick my lips, all of a sudden dying to know what it would feel like to have him in my mouth.

"Do you like what you see, sweetness?" he asks, now straddling my legs. He takes my bound wrists and puts them over his head, resting on his shoulders. "Or do you want more?"

"More," I moan, not knowing what necessarily that means, but only knowing I want anything he will give me.

He removes my hands from around his neck and slowly lowers me down to the bed, placing my still bound hands over my head. He stands back up, discarding his briefs and rolling on a condom before climbing back on the bed.

"No more teasing," he says, his mouth slowly kissing up my body. "I need to feel you, Whitley."

"Yes," I groan, aching to touch him but loving the feeling of my wrists in the belt. "Take me, Jake."

And he does. When he enters me, he takes all of me.

My body. My mind. My soul.

My heart.

This isn't the first time we've had sex since we became official, but this is different. The way he's looking at me, the words we exchanged earlier, the way he's moving inside me right now.

This is it. This is the love he was talking about earlier.

"Jake," I say, hoping I can find my voice. "I love you. I love you so much."

My words must do something to him because in an instant, he is hitting a spot inside of me I didn't know was there, making me explode in an instant. My screams only spur him on, and his thrusts grow from intense to all-consuming as he comes apart inside of me.

That wasn't just sex. That wasn't even just love making. That was branding.

Jake Evans was making me his.

"I love you Whitley McAvoy," he says, undoing the belt and bringing me against his chest. I immediately wrap my arms around him, needing to be as close to him as possible. "You? You're it for me, sweetness. You are it for me."

I can't help but smile as he holds me tighter.

I wasn't looking for love. I was only looking for one night.

Little did I know one dance would change my entire life.

15

JAKE

"YOU ARE THE WORST WINGMAN EVER."

I shoot Trent the finger as he not so subtly checks out every woman that walks into the Nashville bar we are sitting at. I'm also silently cursing out Knox for working this weekend, giving him a convenient excuse to get out of Trent's monthly ask of going to Nashville. Normally, I'd plaster on a smile and let him have his fun. But I can't muster it now. Not when all I can think of is the last time I was at this bar, I was meeting the woman who would change my life.

"Oh, come on. Aren't you having fun?" Trent asks. "I mean, I know you aren't. But your girlfriend was too busy for you this weekend, so you're stuck with my ass."

I hate when he's right. Whitley had an event this weekend that was going to keep her busy. I told her I didn't care, but she insisted that I stay in Tennessee. And that if I waited until we saw each other again, she'd have a special present for me.

I hope it involves the high heels she wore at the wedding.

"Fine," I say as I flag down the bartender for another beer. "What did you have in mind? Another bar? Check out the band across the street?"

This perks him up. "I'm so glad you asked. And no, we don't have to relocate at all. Because I'm thinking that... see those girls over there? I think we should introduce ourselves to them."

I take a glance at the way he's gesturing and immediately know who he's talking about. To say that Trent has a type would be an understatement. So it doesn't take me long to pick out the redhead that he has his eye on.

"Why can't you just go over and say hello? You're a grown-ass man, for God's sake, Trent. Have you ever picked up a woman before without help from me or Knox?"

He waves me off, completely ignoring the fact I just dished out. "Why change something that works? Plus, I think Officer Sexy is a much better ice breaker than me."

This earns him a glare. "No. No Officer Sexy. If you want my help to talk to them, I will do that as your friend. But I'm not some damn party trick you can whip out when you need to."

He holds up his hands in retreat. "Fine. No Officer Sexy. But... will you?"

I roll my eyes and take a long pull from my beer before standing up from my barstool. "One of these days you are going to owe me. Big time."

He slaps me on the back, gently pushing me toward the group of women. "When your mom gets her new roof, just remember I'm the friend that made it happen for you."

I won't admit out loud that he's right. I will also never admit that I'm having more fun on *ForU* than I ever thought I would. I like creating content. I like putting a smile on people's faces. The money part might have been the main reason for starting, but even after I get the money for Mom's roof, I'm still going to make videos.

Maybe use the money to save up for a ring?

The thought hits me like a punch to the gut, though not in a bad way. More like a why haven't I thought of that before way? Whitley is it for me. I know we still have to have some talks—

most importantly, like where we are going to live if we continue to see each other—but I'll go wherever she asks. As long as I'm with her, I'll be happy.

"I'm going to need you to not look like a love-sick puppy right now when you go talk to them," Trent says as he smacks me on the back of the head. "Focus, Evans."

"Fine," I say, making my way toward the group of women. I have done this for Trent hundreds of times in our life. Hell, I think the first time I did, it was in first grade at recess. But for some reason, this time it doesn't feel right. I shake away the feeling as I approach the women, who have all turned toward me.

"How are you ladies doing tonight?"

Their eyes light up, and I think one of them starts shaking a bit. "Oh my God! It is you!"

I look around for a second because I'm not quite sure what they mean. "Excuse me? Do we know each other?"

They all start laughing. "Of course not! But we know you. You're that guy from *ForU!* You're Officer Sexy!"

Oh, holy hell.

"Yes, he is," Trent chimes in, walking up next to me. "Did you guys know his first video was shot right here in this very bar?"

Their eyes go wide like they were just told one of the great secrets of the world.

"Really?" one of the girls says, sliding up next to me. "That is so cool. Do you think I can get a selfie with you?"

I look over to Trent for help, which is a wasted effort. He's already started making his way toward the redhead. Which means I'm now on my own.

"Um, sure," I say as she holds up her camera. There's nothing wrong with a selfie, right? I know I have a lot of followers. I don't want to be known as the asshole who wouldn't even take a selfie when recognized in public.

Except it isn't just one. I swear, all I'm doing for the next half hour is taking selfies with women I don't know—and some are a little more aggressive than others. I think one of them pinched my ass. I know, for a fact, one grabbed my junk, and one other put her number in my back pocket.

I think I liked this Officer Sexy thing a lot more when I was dancing in the privacy of my house. There it seemed like it was another life. Like I wasn't the same person as Officer Sexy. Now? Now the worlds are colliding, and I don't know how I feel about that.

Just as I think things have calmed down and people have got their fill of me, I hear the telltale beat of the song that started all of this. I shoot a look over to Trent, who just gives me a shrug.

"Hey, Officer Sexy! Why don't you dance for us?"

"Yeah! Show us what you got?"

"Yeah, Officer Sexy! Don't be shy! I dare you to show us those moves!"

That last comment comes from Trent, who I immediately shoot a death glare to. When I find him, that motherfucker is wearing a shit-eating grin on his face that I want to punch off. That motherfucker knows exactly what he just did. He said the words I've never been able to turn down.

Except right now, I want to, but I don't know if I can.

There are now at least fifty people gathered around me, all of them cheering me on to dance. How do I say to them "hey, I only dance alone because I have a girlfriend and don't have an audience."

But I don't have to take off my shirt. Or even dance for a person. I can just do a few seconds alone. Give the people enough to say they saw the show, then drag Trent out of this bar and head back to Rolling Hills.

Where I can kill him and know where to hide the body so he's never found.

The cheering for me to dance only gets louder, and I know if I don't start soon, I'll have to explain why the man who dances on social media has sudden stage fright. So I take a few steps away from the crowd and begin doing a couple basic things. I rotate my hips around. Getting a little lower each time. When I'm almost on the ground, I lean back on an arm, letting my hips circle around before I pop myself back up. The moves are pretty tame for me, but it's doing the job. The crowd is going wild.

I let my hips gyrate for a second, prepping myself for my now signature move of my handstand to the ground when the feel of hands on my shoulders stops me. And not just any hands, female hands. I can tell because her nails are digging into me in a way that does not feel good at all.

I honestly couldn't tell you what happens next. I turn to look at who is grabbing me before a woman is grabbing my face and bringing my lips into hers. I'm so stunned that I don't move for a second.

When I finally break away—which hopefully was only a second but could have been a minute for all I know—I feel my world crashing down. The music still playing, but it's like everything else is happening in slow motion.

I see the phones held high, videoing what just happened. I see the girl who just assaulted me with her mouth looking at me like I'm crazy. I see Trent's eyes wide, knowing exactly what I'm thinking.

This video is about to be posted on *ForU*. And there is nothing I can do to stop it.

16

WHITLEY

IS THERE anything better than taking off your bra at the end of a long day?

I don't think there is.

I plop down on my bed, letting the weight of the day roll off me. And today has been a doozy. It was one of those days that if anything could go wrong, it tried to. But at the end of the day, the fundraiser was a success; the organization raised twenty thousand dollars, and I have another successful event under my belt.

But the best part of this event? Most of the work was done remotely and online. The only contact I had with the organization was today's event. Which made me think, could I do this anywhere? Or, more specifically, from Rolling Hills?

The more I think about it, the more I'm thinking I can. Many of my clients are in Birmingham, but it's not a bad drive, especially if I'm only making it a few times a month. Most of the things I'm doing to secure donations are through email or phone calls. And if I take my business more remote, could I expand and work with more organizations? Could I expand to work with places in Nashville?

The thought makes me smile. Maybe this could actually work between us. All I know is that this is a road I definitely need to explore.

After a hot bath.

I strip away my clothes from the day as the bathtub begins to fill. I drop in a bath bomb for good measure as I get out a towel and put my hair up. As soon as the hot water covers me, I immediately feel relaxed.

The only thing that could make me feel better right now is Jake's strong hands rubbing away the aches of the day.

What would it be like if he and I had normal days? He gets home from a shift and I have a dinner for two ready? Or if I came home from a fundraiser and he was there waiting for me with a glass of wine and a foot rub? It all sounds so domestic, cliché, if you will, but that doesn't stop me from imagining it.

It also makes me laugh. Every so often, I can't believe how we met. I mean, how does that happen? I've heard of people meeting at bars before. Heck, that's how Ella Mae met her husband in college. But because he gave me a lap dance? What a story to one day tell our children.

Then it hits me. I still haven't seen the video. I don't know why. I've had plenty of opportunities to. But it just never felt like something I needed to see. I have the mental video in my head, and it's one I replay often.

Maybe it's time I saw it. I mean, it is the video that made Jake *ForU* famous; I should at least check out the role I had in helping.

I wipe off my hands and grab my phone, being careful as to not drop it in the bathwater, I download the app I once said I never would.

It makes me pick out a username, and I jokingly want to make it Officer_Sexy's_Woman, but I don't. Instead, I use the same screen name I've had since high school and begin to search for Jake's account.

It doesn't take me long to find, and within a couple of scrolls, I see the first one. I immediately click on it, and I'm transported back to that night in Nashville. I can still hear his voice the first time he spoke. I remember how good he smelled when he leaned in to whisper to me. I remember the rush of excitement I felt as I watched this man dance in front of me.

The video restarts, and this time, I watch me. I almost don't recognize myself. This girl is carefree. She's living in the moment. She's living her best life.

She's happy.

I can't help but smile. That's what Jake does to me. That's his effect on me. It happened that night, and it's happened every day we've been together since.

He makes me happy.

After the fifth time watching, I scroll away from the video. I almost start watching some of the ones he's posted, but many of those I have seen thanks to Betsy.

I begin to scroll on videos and find myself completely immersed in this app. Some of them are hilarious. Some are heartfelt. Some make me wonder why seeing backs being cracked by chiropractors is so satisfying.

Simply: I have fallen into the *ForU* rabbit hole.

I don't know how long I stay in the bathtub watching videos. I know it's long enough that my water is starting to get cold, and I consider getting out, but when I scroll to the next video, I'm frozen in place.

The bar looks familiar. In fact, it's the bar in Nashville where Jake and I met. I take a closer look, and I have to blink a few times before I realize what I'm watching.

It's Jake. Dancing. In public.

But not the night we met.

I check the video's time stamp, and it looks like it was uploaded less than a few hours ago. I knew he was going to

Nashville tonight with Trent. I just didn't realize that would mean he was putting on a live show.

It's fine. No big deal. He's just dancing. There's no harm in dancing.

As the video plays, I wonder why it has as many views as it does. It's not posted onto Jake's account. In fact, the user doesn't even have a profile picture. But if the likes are any indication, the video is slowly creeping to viral status.

Then I see why.

Jake stands up, his hips moving in that way that drives me and every other woman on that app insane. His movements are taking him back, right into the hips of a waiting woman.

And when he turns around, I have to blink a couple times to see what I think I'm seeing.

She pulls him in for a kiss.

And he doesn't push her away.

In fact, if the video is correct, he kisses her back.

The video cuts off and starts playing again from the beginning, and I can't help but watch it over and over. And every time I get to the part I know is coming, I pray I'm not going to see what I know is coming.

But there it is. As plain as day. Jake kissing another woman. A stranger.

They are strangers. They will never know the real me. You? You are real. You know me. The real me. And you're the only one who gets to see my moves in real life, you get me?"

The memory of that conversation, of his promise, punches me in the gut as I realize what just happened.

Jake kissed another woman. And it's all over the Internet to see.

I drop my phone in the tub, and I'm too in shock to care. I knew something like this could happen. Hell, the night we met was a direct product of him hitting on a stranger in a bar with his stupidly sexy dance moves. Was I so naive to think that he wouldn't do it again?

This is my own fault. I knew this was too good to be true. The only man who I truly let in, the only man who didn't see me just for my last name, didn't actually see me at all.

This is what happens when I let my guard down.

This is what I get for falling in love with a thirst trap.

17

JAKE

YOU HAVE REACHED the voicemail box of Whitley McAvoy...

I throw the phone down onto the passenger seat as I drive what feels like one hundred miles per hour down I-65 on my way to Birmingham.

I need to see her. I need to explain to her that it was all a misunderstanding.

Though if the fact that her phone has been going straight to voicemail is any indication, she has seen it, and that should be my clue that she doesn't want to talk to me.

But it also means she hasn't seen the second video. Which means I don't know if I'm too late or there still might be hope for us.

No matter what, I have to try. I'm not letting some rogue fan girl ruin the best thing that has ever happened to me.

As soon as I realized what happened, I sprinted out of the bar. I don't know how Trent got home. I don't care. All I know is that minutes after whoever that was kissed me out of nowhere, my phone was going crazy with notifications of videos I was tagged in. And sure enough, they were all of the impromptu performance.

And the kiss.

"Fuck!" I yell, stepping on the gas a little faster as I pass the first sign alerting me that I'm nearing Birmingham.

I knew I shouldn't have danced. And I don't even know why I did. Was it the dare? Was it the number of people cheering me on? Being recognized in public for the first time? I don't know if I'll ever know why; I just know that I can't let it ruin what I have with Whitley.

My phone rings, and I hurry and grab it, not even looking to see who is calling.

"Whitley?"

"No, but you have one chance, right now, to explain yourself or I swear to Jesus I will drive to your bum-fuck Tennessee town and rip your testicles off with a pair of pliers."

"Betsy?" I ask, nearly missing the exit to get to Whitley's apartment.

"Yes, it's Betsy, you moron. Or should I say, cheating moron?"

I slam my hand against the steering wheel. "I didn't cheat, Betsy, I swear."

Great. If Betsy has seen it then I know Whitley has. I press down on the gas pedal a little more, now only a few blocks from her apartment.

"That's not what it looks like. And I can't get a hold of her and that girl *never* turns off her phone. Which means you better make this right."

Fucking social media. This is why I was barely on the shit before all this *ForU* stuff happened. It's drama. It's people only showing you things they want you to see.

It's only getting one side of a story, and most of the time, the video doesn't tell you everything that is happening.

Take tonight. No one who watched it knows that I had no idea that woman was behind me. No one knows how quickly I pushed her away.

But I don't care what the rest of the world knows. I only care that Whitley knows that it's not what she thinks.

That is, if she'll even let me explain.

"I'm almost to her place," I say, thanking whoever is watching over me right now that there is a parking spot in front of her building. "I love her, Betsy."

"I know you do. I've never seen her smile like this. And I swear, the next time I see her, she better be smiling."

"If she isn't, I give you permission to do the plier thing. I gotta go."

I hang up and jump out of my car as I sprint toward her building. I punch in the key code and race to the elevator, thankful there is a car ready.

I swear it takes hours to go to the tenth floor, and now that I'm nearing her apartment, I realize I have no clue what I'm going to say.

When I got in my car and raced out of Nashville, I just knew I had to see her. But now that I'm here? All I know is that I'm prepared to do whatever she wants. I'll beg. I'll grovel. I'll delete the app, video, and anything else that is in relation to Officer Sexy.

I'll do it for her. Because I love this girl with everything in me.

I hurry off the elevator, and in five quick strides, I'm knocking on her door.

Please answer... please answer...

"Whitley? Whitley, please. Please, let me in."

I knock again, surely waking up her neighbors, but I don't give a fuck. I know she's here. And I'm not leaving until she lets me in.

"Whitley! Please! I—"

My words are cut off as the door slowly opens, and just at the sight of her, my heart breaks.

She's in a robe that looks like it has seen better days. Her hair is in a jumbled knot on top of her head. Her eyes are bloodshot, and I know I caused those tears.

"What are you doing here, Jake?"

"We need to talk."

"We don't need to do anything," she says, taking a step forward, blocking my entrance. "You made the decision to become a social media magnet for women. You made the decision to take your shirt off and dance for strangers. You made the decision to do it tonight. And you made the decision to kiss that woman. So as far as I see it, *I* don't need to talk about anything."

She's right. This is all on me.

"You're right. This is on me. But if you'll let me in, I'll explain everything. But please, let me explain."

I don't think I breathe for the ten seconds it takes for her to slowly step back, allowing me entrance into her apartment.

"I tried to call you," I say, though I don't know why. Probably because the silence is killing me.

"I dropped it in the tub. Side effect of seeing your boyfriend kiss another woman on social media."

That takes me by surprise. "I thought you didn't have the app?"

She shrugs, sitting down on the couch. "I downloaded it tonight. You see a whole lot of everything on that. Though I didn't expect to see you dancing and kissing other women."

I take a seat next to her, though I make sure to keep a few feet between us. Which kills me just as much as knowing how badly I hurt her tonight.

"Whitley, I will admit. I did dance tonight. It-it happened kind of all of a sudden and next thing you know… well, that doesn't matter. It was stupid and I know it was. I didn't have a good feeling when it happened, and I should have gone with that. But I didn't. As for her, I didn't even know she was behind me. She shocked the hell out of me when she kissed me. I-I didn't know what to do."

"But you didn't do anything," she says, tears threatening as she tries to keep her composure. "You just stood there. You let another woman kiss you. After you." Her words trail off, and I can see the emotion written across her face. "You PROMISED me that this exact thing wouldn't happen."

"I know I did." Unable to resist holding her hand right now. I reach for it, bringing it between both of mine. I let out a sigh of relief when she doesn't fight me away. "And I will never be able to apologize enough for that. But I hope this helps."

I reach for my back pocket and pull out my phone, opening the app that started all of this trouble.

"Jake, I don't want to see it. I've already watched it more times than I care to."

I shake my head, finding the video I filmed and posted somewhere around the Tennessee-Alabama border.

"Please, watch this," I say, handing her my phone. "Watch this. If you still hate me and want me to leave. Then I will. But please, just watch."

She takes the phone out of my hand, and I sit back, listening to my words.

I want to address something that happened tonight in Nashville. I also want to say that this will be my last video I post to this app.

She looks at me, and I nod, signaling for her to keep watching.

Tonight, I was in Nashville with a friend when I was recognized. That in itself is fine. I enjoyed meeting followers. I didn't mind taking photos or talking to the people I met. Then, on a dare that I now regret taking, I was asked to dance the way many of you know me to do on this app. Though I thought I shouldn't, I did. At that moment, a follower, who I had never met, felt that she had the right to put her hands on me and kiss me without my consent. And worse, that kiss didn't just anger me, but I know for a fact that it hurt my girlfriend.

And not just a girlfriend who might be out of my life after a few months, the woman who I one day hope to marry.

I can see the tears pooling again in her eyes. I can only hope they are tears of forgiveness and not goodbye.

Yes, I have a girlfriend. I don't post about her on here because I like to keep parts of my life private and away from social media. But this girl, she's the best thing that ever happened to me. She knows me for me, not the man who dances and takes his shirt off on here. I love her. I only hope she loves me back.

Because right now, I'm not sure. I don't know if I'd forgive me if I saw the video that was taken of me tonight. But my girl has the biggest heart I've ever known. I can only hope she has it in that heart to give me a second chance. I don't care that the video painted me in a bad light. All I care about is that it hurt the woman I love, and I can't let that happen.

So, my friends, this is it. This app has been fun, but if it's going to hurt the ones I love, then it's not for me. Thank you for your love. Thank you for your support. But now I have to go get my girl.

18

WHITLEY

"HOW DID you know I saw it?"

I don't know why that's my first question after watching that. Somehow it just spilled out of my mouth.

"Your phone was off. I had a sneaking suspicion it was because you were pissed at me."

I mean, he's not wrong, but I'm not about to admit that to him.

"Maybe I forgot to charge it."

This makes him laugh. "You carry four portable batteries with you at all times."

I hand his phone back to him in mock anger. The more I sit here, the more I realize that I can't stay mad at him.

Now that I've had time to think about it, I don't know if it was him I was ever mad at. I could tell from the video that she kissed him. Did he pull away in my liking of time? No. But it makes sense that he was shocked. Hell, I probably would be too.

No, what I'm mad about is that I wasn't there. For the fact that I didn't know I had a jealous streak until a few months ago, and it sure is strong.

And right now, all it wants to do is lay claim on this man.

He's mine. And like hell if another woman is ever going to think otherwise.

"Did you mean it?"

"Yes."

I can't help but let out a small laugh. "You don't even know my question."

He puts down the phone and takes my hands in his. "If it has anything to do with what you just watched, the answer is yes. Did I mean it when I said that I was done with that app 'cause I won't let it come between us? Yes. Did I mean it when I said I love you? With all of my heart. Did I mean it when I said I wanted to one day marry you? Whitley, I would marry you tomorrow if you'd have me. I am so sorry, and if you will let me, I'll make it my mission for the rest of my days to make sure you never cry again."

Oh hell, how am I supposed to stay mad at that? Though there are a few things I need to say, and if I don't now, I don't know when I'll have another chance to.

"I hate that another woman kissed you."

"I hate that she did too. Please know she got an earful from me. Of course, that part didn't make it onto video."

"Want to know what I also hate?"

"What's that, sweetness?"

I look down at our hands, taking a second to lace my fingers through his. "I hate that I wasn't there."

That takes him by surprise. "You what?"

Now it's my turn for the speech.

"I love you, but I hate being apart from you," I say, inching a little closer. "I hate that I only get to see you a few days a month. I hate that I feel like our lives are so separate. I hate that when I watched that video tonight, I had even an inkling of doubt that you would cheat on me. I hate that people only know you because you take your shirt off on the Internet. I hate not waking up next to you each morning. I hate only getting to see your face on a screen at night."

"Tell me what to do," he says, kissing each of my hands. "Tell me what to do to make this right and I will."

"Do you have a closet free for me?"

I didn't know I was about to say those words, but now that they are out there, I don't hate that I did. I want to be near him. I want to see him every day. I want our lives to be together, not just when it's convenient for our work schedules.

Not to mention I want every woman in Rolling Hills, Birmingham, and on social media to know that Jake Evans is a taken man.

Wow, I *am* the jealous type.

"Whitley, did you just ask what I think you did?"

I smile, loving just a little bit that I took him by surprise. "I asked if you have a free closet. At least one. I might need two. I have a lot of clothes. And shoes. Oh goodness, you haven't even seen the beginning of my shoe collection."

Jake blinks a few times, still playing this out in his head. "Whitley, are you saying that you want to move in with me? It's been a long night and I'm pretty sure I'm not hearing you correct."

I laugh as I slowly climb onto his lap, immediately wrapping my arms around his neck.

"I think that I need to move in with you. It will just keep you out of trouble if I'm always there."

I don't get an answer. Instead, I get his lips crashing into mine with such force that we fall off the couch. I'd laugh if I wasn't consumed by his mouth. Or his hands roaming up my sides. Or his growing erection that I feel as my legs wrap around him.

I'd love nothing more than to keep this going, but there's one more thing we need to take care of.

"Don't stop," he says, trying to continue to kiss me. "Keep. Kissing."

I laugh, but gently push him away. "We still need to talk about the videos."

This gets his attention. "I already told you, no more videos. It isn't worth it."

I shake my head, bringing him in for one more quick kiss. "No, you aren't done."

"But, I—"

I place a finger over this mouth. "I know you enjoy making them. I know you put smiles on many faces and I know you enjoy doing it. I also know that there will always be rogue fans. Maybe we need to have some ground rules, but I'm not going to be the reason you stop. You love it. I love you. I would never tell you to stop doing what you love."

The words aren't even out of my mouth before his lips find mine again. I meant what I said. I'd never want to be the reason he stops doing something that brings him joy. Do I love the fact that I know that women are always going to be trying to throw themselves at him? Not especially. But I also know that this man is one of the good ones. And I would be a damn fool to let him go because of a few insecurities.

"What did I do to deserve you?" he asks, brushing a piece of hair behind my ear.

"I don't know, but I'm so glad you took that dare."

He stands up before leaning down and scooping me in his arms. "Best dare ever."

THE END

MORE BY CHELLE SLOAN

THE SALVATION SOCIETY

Reformation: A Salvation Society Novel

NASHVILLE FURY SERIES

Off the Record

Off Track

Off Season (Coming Fall 2021)

Off Limits (Coming 2022)

NOVELLAS

Thirst Trap

Off the Market at Christmas (Coming December 2021)

ACKNOWLEDGMENTS

Write a novella they say. It will be easy they say. I don't know who "they" are but they lied.

Whitley and Jake's story was not easy to write. Writing a novella isn't either. But I knew I wanted to write this story. I knew I wanted to tell the story of a sudden social media star that women only wish they knew in real life. But who was his heroine? What is their love story?

Then I remembered Whitley. I always knew her story. I always knew she was the "other" McAvoy. I knew all she wanted was to be loved for who she is. I didn't know then, but she needed Jake.

This took me about two months longer to write than I intended it to, but I'm so happy with the way it turned out. I hope you love Whitley and Jake as much as I do.

The best part about all of this? You haven't seen the last of Jake or the crew from Rolling Hills. #staytuned.

Now, to the thank yous. First and foremost, my parents. I've lost count of how many times I've come to you guys with a change in life plans, and never once have you tried to steer me toward a safe course. You've allowed me to follow my dreams and my path, and for that I am forever grateful. And like always, the free rent is appreciated. Added note: Thanks for not asking too many questions about this whole TikTok thing.

To my family and friends: Your support has been amazing. Many of you have no clue how I ended up here, but that doesn't mean the support hasn't been there. I love you all.

Kelly, you've been with me on this book journey since day one. Not only are you an amazing alpha reader, but you are an amazing friend. Maybe one day we can go on a book trip again.

Julia, Georgia, Mae and Claire: How did I write a book before I met you ladies? All I know is I don't ever want to write one without y'all again. Extra special thanks to Julia and Mae. This book would still be on Chapter 4 if it weren't for you two.

Evie and Jill J., thank you for helping me get this book to the finish line.

Marla, thank you for your detailed eye. One day I'll stop overusing common words. Michele, thank you for catching all the little things and being an amazing cheerleader. Angela and Amanda, thank you for helping make this book the best it can be.

Jill S., thank you once again for being absolutely amazing in helping me promote this book. You're a rockstar. Michelle, thank you for keeping my life in order.

Kari, when I see an email from you that says "I have an idea" I already know it's going to be amazing. This cover is perfection.

Corinne, I'm here because of you. If you wouldn't have given me a chance I wouldn't have started writing. You forever changed my life.

Adriana, thanks for always picking up the phone.

Last but not least: My Book Squad and my Thirst Squad on TikTok, thank you all for coming on this journey with me. This book is for you. I don't know what I did to deserve the love you show me, but I treasure it every single day.

ABOUT THE AUTHOR

Known for her witty sense of humor, Chelle Sloan is a former sports reporter who recently completed her Master's in Journalism, and is now putting that to good use — one happily ever after at a time.

An Ohio native, she's fiercely loyal to Cleveland sports, is the owner of way too many — yet not enough — tumblers and will be a New Kids on the Block fan until the day she dies. She does her best writing at Starbucks, where you can usually find a Pink Drink within reach. Oh, and yes, you probably saw her on TikTok.

As for her own happily every after? Maybe one day...

Stay up to date with all things Chelle by joining her mailing list!

Follow her on social media!
Facebook: Chelle Sloan
Reader Group: Chelle Sloan's Book Squad
Instagram: Chelle_Sloan
TikTok: @chellewritesromance
Twitter: @Chelle_Sloan
Website: www.chellesloan.com

Made in the USA
Las Vegas, NV
28 November 2021